## "I love you, Dawn, and I want to marry you."

"But I need time," Dan continued, his eyes fierce with longing. "Live with me for a year. Then if we still love each other, we'll marry."

Dawn stood there, stricken. "I love you...." The words came out dully. "I'll never love anyone as much. But you don't love me. You probably never did."

He flushed angrily. "I'm not going blindly into marriage again."

"Of course not. You want a test run." She flung the words at him. "And at some point I'd fail. Then you could toss me away without a twinge of remorse."

"You're deliberately twisting my words... putting a price on your virginity...a wedding ring—not to mention fifty percent of the community property!"

Dawn pressed her palms against her temples. *It had only been a dream....*

## Books by Emily Spenser

HARLEQUIN ROMANCE
2668–CHATEAU VILLON
2681–WHERE THE WIND BLOWS FREE

These books may be available at your local bookseller.

Don't miss any of our special offers. Write to us at the
following address for information on our newest releases.

Harlequin Reader Service
P.O. Box 52040, Phoenix, AZ 85072-2040
Canadian address: P.O. Box 2800, Postal Station A,
5170 Yonge St., Willowdale, Ont. M2N 6J3

# Where the Wind Blows Free

### Emily Spenser

## Harlequin Books

TORONTO • NEW YORK • LONDON
AMSTERDAM • PARIS • SYDNEY • HAMBURG
STOCKHOLM • ATHENS • TOKYO • MILAN

Original hardcover edition published in 1984
by Mills & Boon Limited

ISBN 0-373-02681-1

Harlequin Romance first edition March 1985

# CHAPTER ONE

It wasn't until the third tour group of the morning entered the Alamo's courtyard that she spotted him. Finally, thought Dawn, an honest-to-goodness Texas cowhand.

Her drawing of the courtyard was complete except for a human figure to give it scale. She had been waiting for a man who might have resembled one of the defenders of the Alamo back in 1836—a man who looked slightly bigger than life.

There had been other men wearing ten-gallon Stetsons and sharp-pointed, high-heeled boots, but they were obviously city slickers or out-of-state tourists affecting the cowboy look. This one was the real thing.

He stood tall, slim, and ramrod-straight on the edge of the crowd. As a concession to the city environment, he was dressed in the Southwest's version of a suit: tan, narrow trousers with a wide leather belt and silver buckle, and a matching whipcord coat with a pleated back. He hadn't bothered, though, to change out of his work-scarred leather boots or to change the Stetson shading his dark hair and bronzed face for one less dusty or worn. It was a striking face, handsome but weatherbeaten; the face of a man who had definitely spent a great deal of his life out-doors battling the elements.

Fortunately, Dawn wasn't in his direct line of vision, so she could study him unobserved. She selected a hard lead pencil and quickly began to block in his head, his broad-shouldered, lithe torso, and his long, lean legs. As she worked she luxuriated in her sense of freedom— freedom from all the endless chores of the last five years, and most exciting of all, freedom to devote her energies to her art.

Pleased with the outline of her Texan, she picked up a softer lead pencil and began to define and emphasise the figure with darker lines. She drew quickly, knowing the group would pass on in a few minutes and she would lose her model. As she caught the strong lines of his face and well-formed sensual mouth on paper, she sensed that he was lost in his own thoughts and not really listening to the guide.

'It was here on this spot,' said the guide in a well-modulated voice that even reached Dawn where she sat on a bench near the wall, 'that Colonel William Barret Travis drew a line on the ground before his 189 tired and battle-weary men. First Travis told them how hopeless their plight was, then said, "Those prepared to give their lives in freedom's cause, come over to me."'

Dawn paused and glanced up at the guide for a moment. Even though she had heard the prepared speech twice that morning, and had known the story by heart since childhood, it was still thrilling to hear him describe how, without hesitation, every man save one crossed the line. Even Colonel James Bowie, stricken with typhoid-pneumonia, asked that his cot be carried over.

They managed to hold off Mexican General Antonio Lopez de Santa Anna's 5,000-man army for ten days, killing 1,600, before the huge force finally breached the walls, butchering the defenders to the last man. Bowie, his pistols emptied, his famous knife bloody, died on his cot, ringed by bodies. Davy Crockett, another of

America's great frontiersmen, met his end here, too, felled at last while swinging his empty rifle as a club.

The guide didn't mention it, of course, but among the dead was also Dawn's own great-great-uncle, Jack Richards. It was her grandfather's tales of Jack and the Old West that had sparked Dawn's lifelong desire to put those scenes down on paper. Some day, with luck, she would do it in oil or watercolour, not just in black and white.

'The defenders of the Alamo had not died in vain,' the guide continued after a dramatic pause. 'The Texans' smouldering desire for freedom from Santa Anna's tyrannies was inflamed by the deaths of these gallant heroes, and just 46 days later General Sam Houston, with 800 men, launched a furious attack on the Mexican army at San Jacinto. Shouting "Remember the Alamo!" they routed the Mexican army in a matter of minutes. Texas was free and a new republic was born.'

There was a moment of brief silence in the courtyard, a silence eerily filled with the ghostly thunder of battle. 'Ten years later,' continued the guide, 'by Texas's request, the US annexed it as its twenty-eighth state.'

'Where did Davy Crockett die?' piped a little boy, unable to contain himself until the question and answer period. Blue-eyed and freckle-faced, the child was jauntily wearing a souvenir coon-skin hat modelled after the one his hero had worn.

Dawn's Texan smiled in amusement at the boy, and then suddenly looked in her direction and caught her staring at him.

Embarrassed, she quickly averted her eyes. He was so attractive that he probably often caught women staring at him. She thought somewhat unhappily of her honey-coloured hair pulled back into an unflattering ponytail.

And for the first time in ages, she regretted her plain,
dowdy clothes that hid rather than highlighted her lovely
figure and long legs. A man like that certainly wouldn't
take a second glance at her. Fortunately, Dawn reminded herself, ensnaring a man was not on her agenda.
*That* was something she could have accomplished years
ago.

The group was leaving the courtyard, but it didn't
matter; she could finish the drawing from her imagination. Reabsorbed in her work, she darkened some of
the shadows with a stick of black charcoal and put in
highlights with white chalk.

It was really one of her best, she thought, inspecting
the finished product with satisfaction. Laying down her
chalk she looked up casually and was shocked to find the
tall Texan leaning against the wall just a couple of feet
away, relaxed and confident. He had obviously been
watching her finish her drawing. His clear blue eyes were
dancing with amusement.

She flushed, her creamy skin filling with colour. Flustered, she dropped her eyes to her drawing. There was
no use trying to pretend that the drawing wasn't of him,
because she had a definite knack for catching likenesses
of people.

'Not bad . . . not bad at all.' His voice was deep and
husky and he didn't bother to hide his amusement over
her predicament.

'Thank you,' she said lamely. 'I hope you don't mind.'

'Not as long as I'm rewarded.'

'Rewarded?' echoed Dawn, her heart sinking, as she
looked down at the drawing. She had planned to add it to
the collection she needed for art school, but at that
moment she would have cheerfully given away the whole
lot to get rid of this man with the piercing blue eyes that

made her pulse quicken and her knees feel ridiculously weak.

'Yep, rewarded. You'll have to join me for lunch, at least.'

'Lunch?' she said and instantly wished she would stop sounding like an echo chamber. The invitation was more appalling than the thought of losing her work. Obviously, he thought her drawing of him was some kind of come-on to catch his attention. Her golden-brown eyes mirrored her fright, and her colour rose again. 'I'm sorry, I couldn't possibly—'

'Why not?' His voice was now challenging and his brows arched mockingly, but amusement still sparkled in his eyes. 'Do I look that frightening?'

'Of course not,' she said, bridling, as she gathered up her pencils and charcoal and put them in her box. 'It's just that I'm not in the habit of dining with strange men.'

'But it seems to me you know my features rather intimately,' he said sardonically, flashing a glance at her drawing. 'Are you a professional artist?'

'No, I'm not good enough. I hope to be some day, though,' she admitted, looking up at him. 'Would the drawing be reward enough?'

'Nope, not that I wouldn't like it,' he said, folding his arms. She could feel his eyes coolly assessing her. 'Lunch . . . and you may as well agree peaceably.'

Or what? Dawn wondered. 'That's silly,' she snapped. 'Why do you want to have lunch with me, anyway? I imagine you know plenty of females who'd jump at an invitation,' she added, as coldly as she could manage.

At once he grinned ironically at her. 'Hundreds, maybe thousands, but you interest me. Now get your stuff together and stop arguing.' Abruptly his voice had assumed the authoritative ring of a man who is not only used to giving orders, but used to seeing people jump to execute them. 'I won't bite . . . anything that is, but a thick, juicy steak. And I know just the place to get one.'

Dawn felt her resistance weakening at the thought of a steak. She had only allowed herself a coffee and sweet roll for breakfast that morning, and the budget for lunch dictated nothing more than a hot dog at a stand. But that's no reason to accept his invitation, she scolded herself silently. Besides, she resented his imperious manner. Just who did he think he was to order her around? She jumped up from the bench and picked up her supply box and sketch-book.

'I couldn't possibly let someone I don't know buy me lunch,' she said tartly, 'and frankly, I couldn't afford a steak.' She turned to leave.

He moved smoothly to her side and masterfully took her by the arm. Steering her towards the exit, he drawled, 'I've never let a lady pay for her own meal while she's with me, and I'm not about to start now.'

Exasperated, she said grimly, 'You are persistent!'

'Name's Dan Kane,' he said casually as he opened the door to the street for her. 'After you get to know me better you'll find I generally get my way.'

'That wouldn't surprise me,' she responded, 'except that I have no intention of spending more time with you than it takes to consume a meal,' she added, her eyes flashing up at him. She was tall—five feet eight—but he towered disconcertingly over her. Dawn hoped he hadn't heard the slight quaver in her voice. What woman wouldn't be rattled when confronted with six foot four or so of overpowering masculinity who was bent on getting his own way and generally got it!

Dan Kane grinned.

'What's your name?' he asked, after they had walked a block.

'Dawn Richards,' she said tersely.

'Dawn . . . that's a right pretty name. Don't hear a Texas accent. Where do you come from?' he asked, as they entered a restaurant on the river side of South Alamo Street.

'Southern Arizona, near Colbert,' she replied, taking in the scene around her.

Dawn had never been in such a lush interior. Her dining-out experiences had consisted of an occasional meal in Colbert's Koffee Kup, the town's only restaurant. And never had she seen such well-dressed people.

'Colbert,' Dan said. 'Never heard of it.'

Dawn couldn't help smiling. 'That's no surprise, it's a town in southern Arizona with a population of 494 at the last count. Frankly, I think the census taker may have counted a horse or two.'

Dan chuckled as a man in a black suit, an immaculate white shirt, and a stiff, black bow-tie approached them. 'Mr Kane!' he exclaimed, smiling broadly. 'A pleasure to see you.' He seemed to mean it. Dawn began to wonder just who Dan Kane was, besides being her image of a heroic frontiersman reincarnated.

'Morning, Rudy. I hope you have an outside table for us.'

'If we didn't, we'd surely make one for you,' the man responded jovially.

He led them beyond old-fashioned booths and tables elegantly set with gleaming white linens, china and silver, to the outside covered porch. Several women glanced at them as they walked by their tables. Dawn could sense that the contrast between the commanding, handsome man at her side and her own dowdy appearance had stimulated interest. They weren't the only ones who were inquisitive, Dawn thought wryly. Who was this man? Certainly not just a cowhand. He was obviously as comfortable in this posh restaurant as he would be lassoing a steer. And what had made him so set on having lunch with her?

The view from the porch stopped her speculations and took her breath away. Below her, three tiers of umbrella-topped tables cascaded down to the Paseo del Rio, the lovely walkway along the river. Jade green and fresh-smelling, the San Antonio flowed gently by lush and beautifully landscaped banks. As she stood enchanted, a flat-bottomed, bright red river boat crowded with wide-eyed tourists floated by in stately fashion, beneath palm and banana trees.

Stopping at a spacious end table near the river's edge, the head waiter pulled out a chair for Dawn. After they were seated he handed them the large, ornate menus with a flourish. 'Cindy will be your waitress today, Mr Kane. Enjoy your meal now.'

'Scenic enough for a budding artist?' Dan Kane asked, a hint of irony in his voice, after Rudy had left.

'It's beautiful,' Dawn said truthfully. Then, to avoid those mocking blue eyes, she glanced at the menu only to be overwhelmed by the welter of choices—and the prices.

'Decided what you'd like yet?' he asked after a few minutes. Then, sensing her indecision, he added, 'Or would you like me to order for you?'

'Yes, please do,' she said in relief, looking at him fully for the first time. His eyes were gentle, contrasting strongly with the fierce angles of his face and the strong line of his jaw.

'Fine. We'll keep it simple.' He smiled warmly. Under his dominating, arrogant exterior was a natural friendliness that attracted her. She watched him signal their waitress, who also seemed to know him. He couldn't be much older than thirty-six or so, Dawn decided, and he wasn't wearing a wedding ring. Then she chided herself. What was she thinking of? What possible difference could his age or marital status make to her?

'We'll start with tossed salads, Cindy. Then tell Manuel to toss his two biggest T-bones on the grill. We'll have baked potatoes with sour cream and chives.' He turned to Dawn. 'Do you like mushrooms?'

'Yes.'

'Good.' He turned back to the waitress. 'Give us a side of grilled mushrooms and a bottle of one of your California Cabernet Sauvignons.'

'I hope you're hungry,' he said after the waitress had bustled away.

'I am, actually,' Dawn confessed, aware of a crazy mixture of sensations that made her nerves taut. She felt extraordinarily inexperienced and gauche next to this undeniably attractive man. He had taken off his hat, and his dark, thick, slightly unruly hair added to his looks. For the life of her, she was still unable to figure out a single reason why he was about to spend a fortune wining and dining her. Then she decided that, until she could, she might just as well relax and enjoy what was undoubtedly going to be a fantastic meal.

When her eyes came to rest on her companion she found him casually leaning back in his chair and watching her. Dawn could tell he was intrigued. Even in dowdy clothes, and with her face innocent of makeup and her hair pulled back in an unflattering ponytail, she knew that the discerning male eye would find her attractive. Her bone structure was classic, her creamy complexion was flawless, and her features were regular and well-proportioned. But she had encountered few discerning male eyes. Men, she had learned, rarely looked beyond surface-level trumpery and frills. Certainly, a man like Dan Kane wouldn't need to bother. He was the magnetic sort of man women swooned over in droves. Yet, inexplicably, here he was, studying her with those mesmerising blue eyes.

'What brings you all the way from Colbert?' he asked, cutting into her thoughts.

Before she could frame an answer, he added mischievously, 'Besides wanting to draw strange men in the courtyard of the Alamo?'

His impish comment caught her off balance and pierced her reserve. She smiled unselfconsciously at him—a full, wide, beautiful smile. To her surprise he didn't smile back and his eyes turned wary. Really! thought Dawn in exasperation, as she felt the colour rise on her cheeks. If he thought she was being flirtatious, he couldn't be more wrong. Annoyance crept into her tone.

'I wasn't drawing you, actually . . . I mean, it's just that you looked the way I imagined the defenders must have looked.'

He laughed and the wary look faded from his eyes. 'Believe it or not, you're not far off. My great-great-grandfather, Sam Kane, did bite the dust there, and my family always claimed I was the spitting image of him.'

'Really!' she said in delight. 'So did one of my ancestors, Jack Richards!'

'Well, that settles it,' he said, 'and it practically makes us related. This calls for a celebration.'

As if on cue, the waitress arrived with the bottle of wine. Dawn didn't get a chance to ask *what* was settled.

'Don't open it, Cindy. We've changed our mind and we'll have your best champagne.'

The waitress, obviously burning with curiosity, left, but not before flashing a glance at Dawn.

Dan observed the glance and grimaced as soon as they were alone. 'Afraid you may have been added to the list of potential mates for me.' His face darkened briefly. 'Sometimes it seems as if I can't even say hello to a woman without starting a rumour,' he complained. Then, with a flash of irritation he added, 'Don't you women ever think about anything except marrying? Or marrying off any nearby mates who are lucky enough to be loose?'

'Yes, we do,' Dawn retorted with a surge of annoyance of her own. 'Or at least *I* do,' she said tartly. 'I've had to spend the last five years raising three brothers and two sisters, and I assure you marriage is the last thing on my mind. For the first time in my life I'm free to do what I want to do.'

'Which is?'

'Study art. I'm going to the art school here in September.'

The waitress came back with a silver ice bucket clinking with ice, and two frosted, hollow-stemmed champagne glasses. Dismissing her, Dan opened it himself with an expertly muted pop, and filled their glasses with a flourish.

He lightly clinked his glass to hers. 'To Jack Richards, Sam Kane, and the other brave defenders of the Alamo.'

Dawn took a small sip of the pale, bubbling liquid. It was nothing like the too-sweet, sticky stuff she'd tasted once at a friend's wedding. This was luscious—dry, light, and crisp.

'Do you go to the Alamo often?' she asked.

Dan shrugged. 'I like to stop in when I'm in town. It helps me keep my perspective on things,' he said cryptically.

Their salads arrived along with a warm loaf of dark, crusty, home-baked bread, and a large, fluted dollop of butter. They talked while they ate. To her surprise, he was a good listener and a skilful questioner. Before she knew it she was telling him all about herself and her family.

'We only have a small ranch,' she told him matter-of-factly, 'and when my mom died the summer I graduated from high school, we couldn't afford a housekeeper to take care of my younger sisters and brothers. There was nothing for me to do but to take Mom's place until Betty Jean—she's the next oldest—could take over.'

'And you'd wanted to go to art school even then?' Dan asked gently.

'Oh, yes. My application had already been accepted. I was going to start that September.' Dawn spoke calmly, but without realising it, her expression told him far more than she knew. Her soft brown eyes mirrored the devastation she had felt that summer from those twin blows—the loss of her mother and the shattering of a life-time dream; and the determined tilt to her chin reflected the spirit with which she had tackled what had to be done.

'My family was great, though,' she added, in undisguised pride. 'Everyone pitched in on the after-dinner chores so I could have evenings free to study on my own. Somehow, even without instruction, I think I've managed to improve.'

'If the drawing you were working on today is typical,' Dan Kane said firmly, 'I'd say you don't need much instruction.'

'Thank you,' Dawn said, trying not to show her pleasure at the praise.

The flow of conversation was interrupted briefly when the waitress returned, heavily laden with two huge stainless steel plates set in wooden platters. Dawn stared down in amazement at the size of her sizzling steak, appetisingly criss-crossed with grill lines, and accompanied by the potato and a mound of grilled mushrooms.

Dan laughed at the expression on her face, and encouraged her to try the sweet red-pepper relish, a restaurant speciality, on her meat.

They continued to talk, and although Dawn wasn't usually very free-spoken, she ended up telling him a great deal more about herself and her family than she'd ever shared with anyone.

After the meal she was thankful that he ordered a pot of strong coffee to be brought to their table. Her head was too airy, and the novel, warm glow that had spread through her body from being the focus of his attention, was too disconcerting.

'Do you realise,' she said suddenly, 'you know all about me, and I know nothing about you, except that you're . . . unattached.'

'Widowed,' he said in a flat voice.

'I'm sorry.'

'You needn't be. Our marriage had been dead for a long time anyway.' He gave her a wry smile and smoothly diverted attention from himself by saying, 'I know about your background, but I don't know what you plan to do until classes start in September.'

'Work . . . as soon as I find a job, that is,' she answered lightly.

'Would you consider being a companion to a thirteen-year-old girl?'

'Whose thirteen-year-old girl?'

'Mine.'

She gave him a long, searching look. 'Why are you suddenly dreaming up a job for me?'

'I'm not, he said. 'I spent the whole morning interviewing a dreary collection of women—either too old for her or *quite* unsuitable,' he said with a frown. 'I want someone old enough to be in a position of authority over Suzy but young enough to be a companion as well. In fact, someone like you. I felt it the minute I saw you in the courtyard.'

Dawn's heart plummeted. She didn't know why it should disturb her so to find out that Dan Kane's interest in her had been as a potential companion for a daughter. After all, she had known from the start there was nothing about her that would interest a man as magnetically attractive as he was. She forced herself to smile to hide the sudden, irrational ache inside her.

Dan must have misread her expression. He pulled out the business card of a domestic help employment agency. 'This is the outfit that set up the interviews. Why don't you call them if you have any doubts about what I'm offering?'

'So this lunch has been an interview?' Dawn asked.

'You could call it that. Of course, I had no idea whether I could entice you away from whatever job you had. Needless to say, I was delighted to discover you were looking for one.'

'Actually, taking care of a child wasn't exactly what I had in mind,' she said after a brief pause, then added, 'besides, with tuition to save for, I need to make the kind of money a waitress job in a nice place would bring me.'

'I'll find out from Rudy what a waitress makes here and match it,' he said, again with the easy confidence of a man who always gets his way. 'At the end of summer, as a bonus, I'll toss in a year's tuition.'

'A year's tuition?' Dawn was astounded. Although the idea of working for a man who stirred her senses so acutely—without meaning to, or caring whether or not he did—didn't appeal to her in the slightest, the financial side was more than appealing. She could even send some money to her family. It would be stupidity to turn it down.

'My daughter's welfare is very important to me,' he was saying. 'My place is pretty remote. During the school year Suzy goes away to school, but she's home now for the summer. Although I have a housekeeper, she's on the matronly side, and Suzy . . .' he paused, and his voice became more grim, '. . . Suzy doesn't want to be mothered, and she's gotten to be a bit of a handful.'

'They usually do at that age,' Dawn said drily.

'I can't imagine you'd have much trouble, though, and I assure you, you'll have plenty of leisure time for yourself. If you and Suzy hit it off it could be a permanent summer job with the same terms, as long as you're in school.' He leaned forward, his eyes coaxing. 'How about it?'

'I must confess, it sounds too good to pass up,' Dawn responded reluctantly.

'Good, it's settled. I'll pick you up at seven tomorrow morning. What hotel are you staying at?'

'I'm not at a hotel. I have a room at the YWCA.' Suddenly things were moving too fast for her. She felt herself being swept along a potentially dangerous course—one with plenty of rapids ahead. And yet she sensed that any objections she came up with now would be brushed away. It had only taken one lunch to know that Dan Kane did indeed generally get his way.

Deep in thought, Dawn strolled along the Paseo del Rio for a while after he left her. Rivers were novelties in the arid Southwest, and she savoured the cool, unique beauty of the San Antonio.

Just before leaving her, Dan had insisted on advancing her some of her salary, and had handed her a couple of folded bills. After he had left, she glanced down at them and discovered they were hundred dollar bills. She had never seen a real one before, and her first thought was to head for the nearest post office, buy a money order, and send her father back the money he had somehow scraped together for her bus ticket to San Antonio and for her living expenses until she got a job.

'I can only take it as a loan, Dad,' she had said lamely, overwhelmed by surprise when he had handed her the bus ticket just one day after Betty Jean had graduated from high school. 'I know how many other places this could go.'

'You earned it, kid,' George Richards had said gruffly. 'Just don't forget you can always come home if things don't work out.'

But on second thoughts, Dawn realised, continuing to walk aimlessly along the elegant and lovely Paseo, her father might find her explanation of how she came by the money a little hard to swallow. Indeed, he might take the first bus to San Antonio, Grandpa's old rawhide whip in hand, determined to rescue her from a white slaver or worse. She smiled at the image.

Dawn was a good judge of character and she felt Dan Kane was on the level—primly, she repressed a small, silly twinge of disappointment over that. On leaving he had again thrust the card of the employment agency into her hand, and told her they would give him a character reference if she had any doubts about him. No, she wasn't worried about that aspect of her new job, but she decided not to send her father money until her first real paycheck, when she could tell him more details about her new job than she knew now. There would be plenty to send.

At a narrow section of the walk, as she stopped to let a small group of well-dressed, attractive women pass, she caught a glimpse of her reflection in a shop window. She was even more frumpy than she had realised. On impulse she entered the next clothing shop and looked around, barely seeing the coats, jeans, and shirts, until her eyes fell on the racks that held summer dresses and—even more exciting—bathing suits.

Dan Kane seemed well-off enough to have a swimming pool on his ranch, and for some reason she rebelled at the thought of being seen in her four-year-old one-piece. Dawn tried on several bathing suits until she found exactly what she wanted—a brief, lime-green bikini that set off and revealed the shapely lines of her youthful figure. She pulled the rubber band from her hair, and let the honey-coloured tresses, thick and wavy, fall loosely around her face. At the sight of the sexy-looking female staring back at her from the mirror a vague depression lifted, one that had descended when Dan Kane told her that on first sight he saw her as the perfect child-companion—he didn't have to add the words 'nice and dull,' but she knew he was thinking them.

When she walked out of the dressing room, a saleswoman was waiting for her.

'I noticed you trying on one of our new swimsuit lines,' the woman said in a friendly tone. 'Did you see these matching terrycloth coverups? They're quite fashionable.'

The material, closer to velour than terrycloth, was a brilliant white, and the neckline and sleeves were edged with piping of the same lime-green material as the suit. A lime-green tie-belt added a finishing touch. Dawn couldn't resist trying it on, and its casual elegance so flattered her that she found herself buying it, the suit, and a pair of high-heeled sandals. In a heady excitement she had almost been tempted to look for a new dress as well, but there were a few other things she wanted to buy at an art store she'd noticed on South Alamo Street.

By the time Dawn had left the art supply store, she was loaded down with packages. She hadn't realised how many things one needed to paint watercolours, or how expensive they all were. The paints, special paper, and the odds and ends weren't so bad, but the brushes—fifteen dollars for one measly sable brush! And the sales clerk said she needed at least three different sizes to do anything. Fervently, Dawn hoped Suzy wasn't a terror, because now she'd have to last at least a week to earn what she'd just spent.

The next morning she was awakened early by the automobile traffic on the city streets below her third-floor window. It wasn't the sort of thing she'd ever had to become accustomed to back on the little ranch near Colbert. The noise had disturbed her sleep during the night, too, or at least she preferred to think it was that, and not the image of Dan Kane's strong, handsome face with his clear, piercing, blue eyes, which had haunted her dreams.

After settling her bill at the desk, she dismissed the thought of eating—her stomach was too fluttery—and decided to wait outside in the fresh, early-morning air. It was too early for him to be there, but every time she saw a pick-up truck or four-wheel drive vehicle round the corner, her heart leaped. When he finally did arrive, right on time, she was surprised to see he was driving a low-slung, luxury sedan—not the sort of car that would last fifty miles on back country roads.

'Morning,' he said, with an easy smile. His eyes were as piercing as they'd been in her dreams. 'Is this everything?' He gestured at Dawn's two suitcases.

Dawn was ridiculously tongue-tied; all she could do was nod. As it had yesterday, the close proximity of Dan Kane, with his almost visible aura of power and magnetism, played on her senses and made her heart pound. There was a quality of independence about him that she admired. It made her think of a spirited horse—a wild mustang that would never accept a bit and saddle. Like Dawn he was dressed in old jeans, a long-sleeved shirt, and boots. But his, she could see at once, weren't purchased from a mail-order catalogue. They fitted his tall, lean frame to perfection.

After tossing her belongings in the trunk he opened the passenger door for her, then got in on his side.

'Had breakfast yet?' he asked as he swung the car into the heavy flow of traffic, making it look easy.

'No.'

He gave her a warm smile that made her inside smelt. Dawn could tell he was totally unconscious of the effect he had on her. Thank goodness.

'I was going to stop at a restaurant and get us some breakfast before we took off, but I heard there was a storm brewing. So I picked up some sweet rolls and got some coffee in a thermos. Maybe we can beat the storm that way.'

'That will be fine,' said Dawn politely, but she was perplexed. He didn't seem like the kind of person who would fuss about driving in the rain—although with a car like this, they were going to get stuck in the first muddy pothole.

'What's the name of your ranch?' she asked after they had driven a few miles in silence. Like most South-western men, he wasn't given to small talk.

'Rocking K, same as our brand,' he answered, then added, 'It's about an hour and a half trip.'

That didn't sound very remote for Texas, she thought, and was about to say so when Dan turned off the highway towards a small airport. He stopped in front of a rental car office and nodded towards a modern, one-story building next to the airstrip.

'You might want to freshen up while I get rid of this car and turn in my flight plan.'

Flight plan! He must have a private plane, thought Dawn in shock. She looked at him closely. 'Just how large is this ranch of yours?'

'The Rocking K is about seventy-five thousand acres,' he said with an amused smile, sensing the direction of her thoughts, 'give or take a few hundred acres one way or the other. Can't run cattle on all of it though, because of the oil field.'

'How inconvenient,' she replied when she had got her voice back. Seventy-five thousand acres! It had to be one of the biggest ranches in Texas! And an oil field . . . Dawn remembered her grandfather, who had spent most of his life as a cowhand on one Texas ranch or another, claimed that most of the time you couldn't tell a Texas millionaire from a cowboy making thirty dollars a month, unless you saw him at home or driving his custom-designed Cadillac. Or, Dawn now amended, flying his own plane.

## CHAPTER TWO

CLOUDS had begun to form on the horizon, but the sun was still shining over the ranch headquarters when Dan expertly brought the single-engine plane down on the small paved runway near the house.

The flight over the low southern Texas hills had been a thrilling experience for Dawn, and she was sorry to see it end. This section of Texas had none of the desert barrenness of southern Arizona, although there was a beautiful, wild quality about it. Mostly, it was hill after rolling hill carpeted with spring wildflowers, range grasses and mesquite, and sometimes graced with cedar and oak trees. Dawn couldn't help reflecting that if her dad had his spread here he wouldn't have to slave just to get by.

A thin, wiry ranch hand helped her down, then held open the massive door of a large shed near a barn while Dan taxied the plane inside.

'Sam, this is Dawn Richards, Suzy's new companion,' Dan said as soon as the two men, carrying the luggage, rejoined her. 'Sam's the foreman,' he explained, 'and you can always go to him with any questions when I'm not around.'

Sam briefly rested one of the suitcases on the ground while he doffed his hat in her direction. 'Nice to meet you, ma'am.' She judged him to be about sixty, and she liked his open, weathered face. His voice was gruff but friendly, and he responded to Dawn's shy greeting with a gentle smile.

He picked up the bag again, and the three of them started for the low-slung, stucco-covered adobe house. From the air Dawn had seen several wings, three patios and one very large courtyard with a swimming pool, so she knew it was much bigger than it seemed from ground level. She marvelled at the harmony with which the house blended into the surrounding terrain. The grounds immediately surrounding the house were land-scaped with low native palms and rows of red and white oleanders.

'It looks like it's going to rain any minute,' said Dan to his foreman. 'Where's Suzy?'

'Out riding with Slats. We didn't expect you back for another hour or so.'

Dawn was relieved to see that Dan had a healthy lack of concern over the prospect of his daughter being caught out riding in the rain. At least he didn't keep her packaged in cotton wool, she reflected. Nevertheless, she was feeling increasingly nervous about the approaching first meeting with her charge. Would she have any chance at all of developing a good relationship with a child raised in an environment so far removed from the scraggly, bare-bones ranch on which she'd lived all her life?

Hannah was on hand to meet them in the large atrium that served as an entry hall. Dawn barely heard her introduction to the matronly housekeeper, because she was so busy marvelling at the room's visual impact. A massive skylight, through which she could see the great, gathering clouds, made her feel as if she were still outside, and abundant ferns and ivies that spilled from hanging baskets heightened the effect. There were broad-leafed philodendrons in wooden tubs, and here and there, African violets added their brilliant, exotic colour. It was as if she were standing in the loveliest of glades.

'I expect you'll want to wash up and rest a bit before lunch,' Hannah said kindly. 'I'll show you to your room.'

She led Dawn down a long, glassed-in hall that ran the length of the south wing. Dawn had never seen anything remotely like the elegant simplicity of the architecture—except in magazines, and the atrium had only been a foretaste of things to come. White stucco walls and large expanses of glass gave the house an airy beauty, austere but graceful, and brick floors and handcrafted dark wood furniture provided warmth and colour. Green plants were everywhere. In the rooms they passed, she caught glimpses of beautifully placed Indian and Mexican pots and baskets, as lovely as the ones she'd seen in the museum in Tucson.

'I've given you this room in the guest wing, away from the family quarters, so you'll have a bit of privacy when you need it,' said Hannah, leading Dawn into a spacious bedroom. A big Mexican blanket with red geometric designs on a blue field served as a bedspread. Her artist's eye noted with approval that its colours were repeated in the profusion of throw pillows at the head of the bed, and the three huge floor cushions placed near the small, oval corner fireplace. It was the far wall, though, that made her catch her breath. All glass, it looked out on an astounding view of hills and sky.

'What a magnificent view . . . and a beautiful room,' said Dawn, smiling gratefully at the housekeeper. 'I've spent my whole life sharing a bedroom with sisters. It will be lovely to have some privacy.'

'I'm from a big family, too,' Hannah said. 'I imagine you'll enjoy the private bath as well. It's the second door there.'

'It'll be heavenly. Thanks so much.'

'I'm glad you're here, Dawn,' Hannah said, giving her a motherly pat on her shoulder. 'It will be good for Suzy to have someone nearer her age than I am.' She paused, then added, shaking her head, 'I confess, today's kids shock me, but I'm sure you'll manage just fine. Lunch is in an hour.'

Just after Hannah left large raindrops began to speckle the glass. Dawn opened the sliding glass door briefly so that she could smell the heavenly fragrances that were magically released as soon as rain hit range grasses. Soft, fluffy grey clouds, their edges brushing the hills, were massed overhead, and, as Dawn watched, the drizzle turned into a steady downpour. Rain always excited Dawn. Probably, she thought wryly, because the Southwest never got enough of it.

Vague ideas of how she was going to try to capture clouds like those in watercolours began to form in her mind. If she stayed long enough to paint, that is. Hannah's comment on young people today—specifically meaning Suzy Kane, Dawn was sure—did not bode well.

She had finished washing and was drying her hands when she heard a knock at the door. A young girl with long straight brown hair, wet and plastered to her blue shirt, poked her head in.

'May I come in?'

'Sure. You must be Suzy.'

'Uh-huh. I couldn't wait to meet you,' she said, eyeing Dawn frankly. 'Do you need some help unpacking?' It was hard to tell if the offer was sincere.

'Not really,' said Dawn, meeting her cool gaze head-on. 'But why don't you sit down and keep me company while I do it?'

Suzy, who had Dan Kane's colouring but not his good

looks, had a plain, slightly too-narrow face that the long hair only emphasised. Her gawky, leggy look she might or might not lose as she matured, but she could certainly use some work on her posture. As she settled herself among the pillows on the bed, Dawn pulled out a towel from the linen closet in the bathroom and tossed it to her.

'I see you got caught out in the rain,' she said. 'Your hair's dripping wet.'

Suzy caught the towel with a grimace. 'I need a companion, not a mother.'

'Oh,' said Dawn non-committally, remembering Dan Kane's similar comment. She added, not quite truthfully, 'Actually I was thinking about the lovely blanket you're sitting on.'

Slightly disconcerted, Suzy was silent for a moment, then asked bluntly, 'Did my dad tell you about my mother? About how after she married him for his money, she split and took him for every cent she could get?' Suzy picked at the thick towel. 'She managed to spend it all, too, before she got killed in that car crash.'

Dawn managed to hide her dismay over Suzy's precocious cynicism and unemotional account of her mother's death. 'No, I only knew that he was a widower,' she said evenly, as she opened a suitcase and began to put her underwear in the bureau drawer.

'After she left him she joined the jet set. For a while I lived with her: Monte Carlo . . . Costa del Sol . . . the Riviera. Then she got tired of hauling a kid around with all the other baggage.' Suzy paused and gave Dawn a knowing little smile. 'I think I interfered with her extra-curricular activities.'

No wonder Hannah had been shocked! Dawn didn't allow Suzy to see that she had managed to shock *her* to the core, too. But a single glance at the girl revealed so much forlornness and insecurity in those hunched shoulders that Dawn knew the child was only doing it for effect.

Hard-hit by her mother's rejection and death, she probably worked at alienating everyone with whom she came into contact before they had a chance to accept her. That way she didn't have to fear rejection, at any rate. No, thought Dawn, pitying her, not rejection— only loneliness. Dawn despaired at the size of the task before her. Both Dan Kane and his daughter were wrong; this child definitely needed mothering.

'It must have been unpleasant for you,' Dawn said simply.

'Oh, not really,' Suzy lied, her voice giving her away. 'We never heard from her again. The French police let Daddy know about the accident. But that's life, isn't it?' It was an airy, rhetorical question, not requiring a reply. Dawn wondered if that was the way her mother used to talk.

Maintaining a placid expression, Dawn looked up from her unpacking and was slightly cheered to see that Suzy had started to towel dry her hair.

'And now, Daddy's got me rusticating in the sticks among a bunch of hicks,' Suzy said in a dramatic drawl, emphasising the rhyming words.

Again, it was a little too arch, a little too grown-up. Dawn stopped putting the clothes away for a moment and looked askance at her. 'Is that your phrase or your mother's?' she asked quizzically.

Dawn seemed to have struck the right note, because Suzy suddenly looked like the thirteen-year-old she was. She even giggled.

'It was something Mom used to say. Actually, I love

living here, and I wish Daddy wouldn't send me so far away to school,' she said, unconscious of the wistfulness in her voice.

Obviously, her father's attention during three months of the year wasn't enough to allow Suzy to develop a sense of security. From the beginning of the conversation Dawn had been wondering why Dan Kane, who seemed like a devoted father, packed his daughter off to a distant boarding school in the East.

'Aren't there any nearby boarding schools you could go to, so you could at least come home on weekends?'

'Yep, the one all the cowhands and small ranchers send their kids to. But Daddy wouldn't dream of letting me go *there*!'

'Why not?'

'I don't know—he never says,' the girl responded, shrugging her thin shoulders. Her voice turned forlorn again. 'I guess he likes getting rid of me too.'

'I find that hard to believe,' responded Dawn stoutly. 'Of course, I don't know your father very well, but he looks to me as if he cares a great deal about you.'

'Well, you sure can't tell it from the way he zips me off every September, come hell or high water,' retorted Suzy, refusing any comfort.

Until Dawn could find out for herself what Dan Kane's motivation was, she decided, she'd better change the subject. She also tucked away the thought that she'd have to try to do something about Suzy's language. 'Have you made friends at the school?'

She realised it was an unfortunate question as soon as she asked it, because Suzy's expression instantly turned bleak. For a while, at least, talking to Suzy was going to be like walking through a pasture peppered with land mines.

'Who'd want to hang around with an awkward ugly duckling like me?' said Suzy harshly, obviously mimicking someone—her mother again probably. Dawn found herself growing increasingly annoyed with a woman who'd been dead for three years.

'All thirteen-year-old girls see themselves as ugly ducklings,' Dawn responded lightly. 'You can't tell if you'll turn into a swan or not at your age. And looks aren't everything, anyway, believe me.' Sometimes they're even a handicap, she added to herself.

'Well, all those stuck-up Eastern girls who go to that horrible Seaborne Girls' Academy have already turned into swans, and they can't stand me.'

Dawn smiled. 'Somehow, I'd be willing to bet you haven't given them a chance.' Suzy shrugged non-committally. 'I'm dying to see some of the ranch,' said Dawn after a pause, deciding it was time to terminate the conversation. 'If it stops raining, I'd love to take a ride after lunch.'

Suzy's face actually lit up, and she swung her legs to the floor. 'Great! I could ride all day. I'd better go change for lunch.'

She walked to the door and opened it. Turning back she smiled shyly and, to Dawn's surprise, said, 'It'll be nice to have someone to do things with this summer.' Then she left before Dawn had a chance to say a word.

The rain stopped when they were half-way through lunch, which Suzy and Dawn ate by themselves in the large formal dining room. After fortifying themselves with Hannah's hearty chili and beans, and home-baked wheat bread, they made their way to the corral. Dawn was impressed by how competently the girl caught and saddled her thoroughbred quarter-horse Tandy, a stallion with more than a little spirit. Mounted, Suzy lost all her awkwardness. Indeed, she looked as if she'd been born in the saddle.

Dawn passed up the other thoroughbreds in the corral for a less flashy but handsome brown horse with white spots. Something about the wily look in his eye, and the powerful, sure-footed way he moved, made her think he was half-mustang. Suzy confirmed it as they rode towards the low hills to the west.

'Paint's half-Appaloosa and half-mustang. Sam will sure like your choice of horses. According to him, he's one of the smartest horses on the Rocking K.'

Dawn had always loved mustangs, the hardy descendants of those proud horses that had first been brought to the New World by Spanish explorers. Some of them had escaped and run wild for centuries, finding the rugged range to their liking. Then, during the depression in the 1930's other breeds had been turned loose to forage for themselves when their owners could no longer feed them. Gradually the horses interbred with the mustangs, and the resultant half-breeds became known for their intelligence and stamina.

'Was Paint born here on the Rocking K?'

'Uh-huh, he was rounded up when he was just a colt.'

'Rounded up? You mean you still have herds of wild mustangs on the ranch?' Dawn asked incredulously. In her part of Arizona they had all been captured and tamed years ago.

Suzy laughed. 'You make it sound so romantic. But there are so many of them they're pests. If we didn't have a roundup of the new colts every year—and they aren't easy to catch, either—there wouldn't be enough forage left for the cattle.'

Dawn was amused by the note of adult pragmatism in Suzy's voice. And she was pleased on another level, glad she had come to Texas to study Western art. She had been right in thinking it would be easier to capture the flavour of the old days in the state her grandfather had been born in—a state that still had more than a few remnants of the frontier.

'When's the roundup?' Dawn asked.

'The last week in August,' replied Suzy, 'just before I leave for school, so you'll be able to see it.'

Conversation was halted when Tandy, friskily pulling at the reins, grew impatient with the slow, plodding pace.

'Race you to that oak tree,' called Suzy, giving Tandy his head.

It was an uneven match; Dawn had the distinct impression that Paint's willingness to race was no more than a polite overture to a silly stranger who didn't know there wasn't any point to galloping, unless you had somewhere sensible to gallop to. But it was fun to be tearing after Suzy. This job was going to have lots of compensations, she thought, exulting in the smell of the rain-freshened grasses and the cool wind in her face.

But by ten o'clock that evening things were very different. She wasn't sure she had a job any longer, and if she had, she certainly didn't want it. She had lingered in the living room after Suzy went to bed, hoping to have an early and frank talk with her employer about his daughter. Dan and his foreman, however, spent the evening in a small study off the atrium, working on ranch accounts, and planning the next week's activities. Sleepy after the long day, Dawn had just about given up waiting, when she heard Sam leave by the front door.

She looked up to see Dan walk into the living room, and the sight of him started her heart hammering. 'Dawn Richards,' she said sternly to herself, 'you're grown up.

You are *not* to allow yourself to become unhinged by the mere physical presence of this man. Attractive as he may be.'

'Still up?' he asked in surprise, when he saw her sitting on the sofa near the fire.

'Yes, I thought perhaps we could talk,' she said timidly. Dan Kane seemed cold and aloof now that they were alone in the middle of the vast territory he controlled, and suddenly she was shy about opening up so personal a subject.

His brows rose and his eyes grew wary. Without answering, he walked over to the bar and poured himself a drink. Then, slowly, he added a splash of soda from a syphon.

'Would you care for something?' he finally asked, glancing back at her.

'No, thanks.'

Dawn watched him plant himself near the fireplace. He towered over her, leaning one arm against the massive wood mantel. 'I hope you aren't unhappy already,' he said wryly, after taking a sip of his Scotch.

'Not at all,' she said. 'I seem to have hit it off with Suzy . . . I think.'

His face relaxed a little. 'That's my impression, too. I've never seen her take to anyone so fast.'

'She seems to me to be an awfully insecure and lonely child,' Dawn said, her nervousness pushing her tactlessly into the heart of it, 'and somewhat mixed-up.'

His face stiffened as if she were accusing him of child neglect. Well, in a way she was, thought Dawn, ploughing ahead. 'She's not even sure of your love—although it's quite apparent you love your daughter very much.'

'For someone who's known Suzy exactly twelve hours—' He looked at his watch. 'Make that eleven,' he drawled sarcastically, his blue eyes glacial, '—and for somebody who's not a child pyschologist, you're sure damn forward with your opinions.'

'It doesn't take a psychologist to see how insecure your daughter is.' Dawn retorted, heating up. 'Did you know she's afraid you send her East every year just to be rid of her? There's a good boarding school near San Antonio, isn't there? If she went there she could easily get back here on weekends and holidays. It would probably make all the difference in the world.'

He was silent, a moment, staring into the amber liquid in his glass. 'No,' he said quietly, 'it's absolutely out of the question.'

'Why? Is there something wrong with it academically?' She was amazed at her effrontery and persistence. Obviously, he didn't want to discuss it, and it really wasn't any of her business.

'Not that I know of,' he said, in an oddly ominous tone.

'Then, why not?' she asked. She had never been so assertive, and Dan Kane was hardly the sort of man to cross lightly, but it seemed important.

He slammed his drink suddenly on the mantel, making her jump. 'Why? I'll tell you why,' he said harshly. 'My daughter's not going to school with a bunch of penniless cowhands' sons. She's not going to be an easy mark for any young drifter who finds out she's got money.'

'And the chance of somebody getting some of her money—in the distant future—is more important to you than her happiness,' she retorted, almost without thinking, while inside she weathered his insult—indirect, but no less painful for that. His words 'bunch of penniless cowhands' sons' spoke volumes about what his attitude would be towards penniless ranchers' daughters, if she were ever stupid enough to let herself fall for this infuriating, wildly attractive man.

'It's not the money,' he said roughly. He picked up his drink and sipped it. When he spoke again, his voice was husky. 'I won't have her go through the hell of loving someone who only pretends to care about her, while all the time he's coolly calculating her worth in dollar signs.'

Dawn could see how deeply he must have been hurt by his first marriage, but she could also see that there was a hole in his logic. 'But don't you see that's exactly what you're doing?' she said, jumping up to confront him, her eyes flashing. 'You're measuring a person's worth by how much money his family has. I assure you, plenty of poor people wouldn't dream of marrying for money. Sure, that might happen to Suzy, but she might also fall in love with some perfectly honourable man. Life's full of chances.'

'Young woman, you're the most ornery, presumptuous . . . !' Dan clamped his mouth shut, but she could see his powerful jaw muscles working. He was trying hard to keep his temper in check, but his patience was beginning to fray. His eyes flickered over her. 'I don't believe,' he said evenly, 'in taking any more chances than I can help, either for myself or my daughter.'

Dawn was stymied. His voice was like steel. Nothing she had said had had the slightest effect on him.

'I wish you luck then, Mr Kane,' she said. 'May you never have the misfortune to fall in love again.' She didn't bother to try to hide the sarcasm in her voice. 'It might make you human, and I'm sure you wouldn't like that!'

'You don't have to worry about that, Miss Richards. I won't. It's quite easy to avoid, really. I just don't allow women I find too attractive—' he halted. At least he had the grace to flush, Dawn thought.

'—to spend too much time on the Rocking K,' she said, finishing his sentence for him. 'I suppose some of the women you interviewed at the employment agency were unsuitable for just that reason. How lucky you stumbled on me.'

'I didn't mean to insult your looks—on purpose, at any rate. You wouldn't look half bad if you didn't dress so damn dowdy and wear your hair in that ridiculous ponytail,' he said, glowering at her.

'This discussion seems to have been sidetracked. It's now rather pointless, isn't it?' She moved past him to leave, but he reached out and grabbed her arms, his grip like iron.

'Is it? You have the nerve to criticise me about the way I lead my life, and yet you're only twenty-three years old and you already look like an uptight old maid. Why? Taking your mother's place didn't mean you had to make yourself into a frump. There has to be another reason for it. Are you afraid of men? Afraid of life?' he taunted. The unconcealed mockery in his tone made her blood simmer. 'Afraid of taking a chance on love?'

'Not at all,' she responded icily and not quite truthfully. 'I just happen to want to devote my energies to art at this point in my life.' Not only did the words sound ridiculously pompous, but he was quick to see the hole in her logic too.

He lifted an eyebrow sardonically. 'I forgot for a moment. You're an artist, and artists are known for their monk-like lives, aren't they?'

She blushed as he made fun of her. Seething with indignation, she said fiercely, 'Will you please let me go?'

He gave her a sharp, angry smile. 'I'd even hazard a guess that you could be downright attractive, if you wanted to.' He studied her insolently, letting his gaze drift over her body and then rest openly on her face. The sudden, hard intensity of his look frightened her, and she struggled in his powerful grasp. He held her easily. 'Anger suits you,' he said slowly. 'It puts amber sparks in those brown eyes of yours.'

She sputtered with rage. 'Really! Mr Kane, this conversation is getting ridiculous.'

'I don't think you know the first thing about life,' he went on, as if she hadn't spoken, 'or men . . .'

He pulled her towards him. She was too stunned to resist as his mouth crushed down on hers, parting her lips ruthlessly. His hands, their grasp strong but not brutal, held her prisoner. She knew that his mere presence in the room stirred her senses acutely, but she still wasn't prepared for the impact of his sexual power on her. She had never experienced such an emotional onslaught. Her head swam, and she couldn't help the nebulous, primitive response that stirred deep inside her as his demanding lips drank from hers.

When Dan released her at last and stepped back, she was completely dazed, her mouth stinging. Opening her eyes she looked at a taunting smile and scornful blue eyes.

'That should rattle your sweet virginal dreams, Miss Richards.'

Wordlessly, she fled.

Dawn's cheeks were still stained red when she reached her room. She momentarily debated whether she should pack that night or leave it till the morning. Feeling drained and exhausted, she decided to put it off, and changed into her night clothes. Turning off the light, she slipped between the covers, trying to will herself to forget what had just happened and go to sleep, but it was no use. She kept turning the scene over and over in her mind. How unexpected it had been when Dan Kane spun on her and accused her of being a hypocrite. And that kiss—!

She was both surprised and confused by the flood of emotions and memories he had stirred up in her. Hot tears rushed to her eyes. What he said about her was true. She, too, was afraid of taking chances. Dawn had been running from her physical self—and men—ever since she was seventeen. Was it only six years? It seemed a lifetime.

But why, she asked herself, should it make any difference to her if Dan Kane thought her a coward? To be honest she didn't know why. About the only thing she knew at that moment was that she felt like crying. And the last thing she wanted in the whole world was ever to set eyes on Dan Kane again.

# CHAPTER THREE

SHE tossed restlessly through the night and finally fell into a shallow sleep a little before dawn. Early sunlight flooding the room awakened her; she had forgotten to draw the drapes the night before. For a few moments she lay there as the previous night's scene flashed through her mind. She cursed herself for her lack of tact and for that maternal instinct that got her meddling in something that wasn't any of her business in the first place. Her cheeks flamed as she relived the kiss. The thought of having to face Dan Kane in the clear light of day was almost more than she could bear. But lying there, she decided, wasn't going to increase her courage or get her back to San Antonio.

She dressed hurriedly, hoping to find Dan Kane and make arrangements for her departure before Suzy got up. If only she could simply leave a note and not have to face him. But that was impossible, she thought forlornly, her stomach churning. She heartily wished she hadn't spent all that money on that crazy buying spree; now she was unemployed and in debt, too!

Out of habit she started to put her hair back in a ponytail, then halted. Freed, her naturally wavy, honey-coloured hair altered the shape of her face, softening her high forehead and accentuating her slender throat and the sloping curve of her cheeks. That prim look was utterly gone. She almost decided to leave her hair loose, until she realised Dan Kane might think his rude remarks had had an effect on her. And she was darned if she'd give him that satisfaction, even if he was right. Quickly she caught her hair and secured it tightly with the familiar rubber band.

Fortunately, Suzy wasn't up yet, and she found Dan breakfasting alone in the dining room.

Bracing herself, her heart thumping wildly as his piercing blue eyes met hers, she mustered a cool tone.

'Good morning.'

'Morning, Dawn. You're up bright and early.' The casual friendliness of his reply was disconcerting.

'I thought you might want to get me to San Antonio early, so—'

'Don't be ridiculous. You're not going anywhere,' he said firmly. 'Sit down and have some coffee.' He poured her a cup out of the silver warmer.

'If you think for one minute—'

'You take it black, as I recall.'

Dawn bristled at the note of dry amusement in his voice as he interrupted her a second time. Before she could reply Hannah bustled in with a plate heaped with bacon, eggs, country fries, and biscuits.

'I heard you up, Dawn,' she said. 'Here's your breakfast. Sit right down and eat it while it's hot.'

Temporarily defeated, Dawn sat down. She had no quarrel with Hannah. After checking to make sure they had enough coffee, the housekeeper left. Dan calmly heaped some home-made blackberry jam on his biscuit, then looked at her, his eyes glittering with sardonic amusement.

'Actually, I do owe you something of an apology for flaring up like that last night. I don't usually lose my temper so easily. It would be quite a blow to my daughter if you left.' Even when he was apologising he had a way of sounding infuriatingly arrogant. Not to mention the fact that he seemed to be forgetting about that humiliating kiss.

'But as you pointed out last night, I was only with her for twelve hours,' Dawn responded haughtily, her eyes stormy. 'Or was it eleven? I'm sure you can find someone to replace me quickly enough. I don't think she'd be much affected.'

He blandly ignored her words. 'Although I still think the Seaborne Academy is the best school for her, I'll certainly set her straight on why I send her there . . . You really should eat; your food's getting cold.'

'I'm quitting, Mr Kane, right now,' she said, growing more furious by the second. 'I don't want to spend one more night under your roof after the way you . . . after what happened last night.'

'If you're referring to that kiss,' he drawled, his voice suddenly sarcastic, 'I'd have thought you'd take it as a compliment.'

'Compliment!' she gasped, trembling with rage; he was merely toying with her. 'Either you fly me to San Antonio right this minute, or I'll demand that one of your men drive me.'

He gave a short, hard laugh, and his eyes grew flinty. 'You'll find out very quickly my word is law on the Rocking K. You don't go anywhere unless I say so.' Changing to a condescending tone he added, 'Stop being silly. You're perfect for the job and you know it. Otherwise Suzy wouldn't have confided in you so quickly.' His mobile features adopted a placating expression that didn't fool Dawn for a second. He was laughing at her under his breath. 'You really have no valid reason to quit. And if it will make you feel better, I assure you I have no intention of ever kissing you again. I'm not taking any chances—' For a moment his voice had grown hot and intense, but he caught himself in mid-sentence. 'I prefer my women less inhibited and more sophisticated,' he said coolly.

Dawn's cheeks grew hot. He was adding insult to injury. In turmoil and at a loss for words in the face of his incredible insolence, she watched him calmly finish his coffee.

'You can come over to the working corrals with Suzy today,' he said as if she were a child, and he were offering her a treat if she finished her vegetables. 'We're bringing in another herd off the range today. Bring your sketch book. It can be pretty colourful.' His smile as he left the room was one of overbearing confidence.

The way Suzy's face lit up when she came in just a few minutes later and saw her sitting there ruined Dawn's half-baked plan to steal a car—or at least a horse—and make her way back to civilisation. It pained her to admit it, but Dan Kane was right. His daughter had taken to her, and would read her departure as rejection. Somehow, much as she hated Dan, and much as she rebelled against the idea of giving in to him, she knew she didn't have the heart to hurt this vulnerable young girl. Besides, she forced herself to remember, there were practical considerations, such as the bonus of a year's tuition. It probably wouldn't kill her, Dawn finally decided in glum resignation, to spend twelve weeks on the same ranch as Attila the Hun—as long as he kept his promise about keeping his hands to himself.

Spring roundup on her father's spread was always a small affair, spanning two days or so, and had been over for weeks. It surprised Dawn to find out it was still in full swing on the Rocking K. She could hardly believe it when Sam told her that it had been going on since mid-April.

'That's six weeks,' she said, startled. She and Suzy were sitting with Sam on the fence of one of the working corrals.

'Yep,' Sam grunted.

'There must be thousands of cows on the Rocking K,' Dawn exclaimed.

'Yep. We got a few,' drawled Sam, as he removed his hat and scratched his head. He put it back on, and took a great deal of time adjusting the tilt of the sweat-stained brim. Dawn was discovering that not all Texans were tellers of tall tales. Some, like Sam, delighted in a tongue-in-cheek understatement.

'How long's it going to take you clowns to catch that silly varmint?' he bawled suddenly at three cowboys who were struggling to corner a particularly rambunctious calf.

Dawn and Suzy grinned at each other. It was thrilling to sit there and watch the frenetic scene of cowboys attempting to separate the calves from their mothers. The cowboys always won in the end, but it wasn't an easy task, especially with these huge, frisky, half-wild cattle that were nothing like the placid Herefords Dawn was used to. To be honest, thought Dawn, she wouldn't have wanted to work with them, even though they would bring a better price at market, with the extra meat they carried. They were obviously dangerous and hard to handle.

She had to confess, though, that Dan Kane, astride a coal-black stallion, looked as cool and collected as if he were handling a herd of milk cows. His tall, dominant figure was everywhere, especially if any of the crew ran into trouble. At one point, her heart almost stopped in fear for him (not that she would have admitted it) when a belligerent steer charged him. Deftly, man and horse working as one evaded and lassoed the creature before it knew what had hit it. Dawn smiled wryly to herself. No wonder she hadn't stood a chance that morning. Just watching the smooth way he and his men worked as a team made her understand why he laughed when she said she'd have one of them take her to San Antonio. His word *was* law, not because he paid their salaries, but because his men respected and admired him. That was the kind of loyalty that couldn't be bought, but only earned. Dawn was impressed in spite of herself, doubly so because with all his money and power he worked as hard as—if not harder than—the hands.

'How much longer do you think the roundup will take, Sam?' asked Suzy, breaking Dawn's reverie.

'Couple of weeks. Why?'

'Could we go with you when you move the herds up to the summer range?' she asked excitedly.

'Nope. You know your daddy's not going to let you go on a cattle drive.'

'But I have Dawn to go with me. Come on, *please*, Sam. You could talk Daddy into it.'

'Ain't you forgetting about that fancy house-party?' Sam appeared unmoved by Suzy's pleading, but his eyes twinkled. 'You know we leave while it's still going on.'

'Yuck,' said Suzy, her face falling. 'I forgot about that.'

'What house-party?' asked Dawn curiously.

Suzy frowned. 'Daddy always throws a big party for his Petrol Club friends after spring roundup.'

'The Petrol Club? That's an odd name for a club.'

'You have to be an oil millionaire to join,' responded Suzy with a grimace. 'Some of them are okay, but I hate it when they all bring their wives and stuck-up kids.'

All kids were stuck-up to Suzy, Dawn reflected. She would have been willing to bet that they in turn found Suzy clumsily shy.

'Some of them ain't that bad,' said Sam, 'but I have to admit I wouldn't mind tossing one or two of those youngsters into a waterhole. Filled with mud.'

Suzy giggled. She turned to Dawn. 'He means Ted Johns, I bet. He's eleven. Last year he put a snake in Sam's bed.'

Dawn shuddered. 'How awful! It was a harmless one, I hope.' She herself had a terrible fear of snakes, of which she had unsuccessfully tried to cure herself.

'Well, sure,' said Suzy, grinning, 'or else Sam wouldn't be here.'

'Well, that little whippersnapper just better not try that little trick again, that's all I can say,' retorted Sam. 'Tell you what, Suzy. I bet you might be able to talk your daddy into a campout sometime this summer, now that you got Dawn here. If she's agreeable, I'll drop a word in his ear . . . pave the way, so to speak.'

Suzy got so excited she almost fell off the fence.

'I'd love it,' said Dawn, laughing. 'That is, *if* you talk him into it.'

The days of the roundup fell into a relaxed, easy pattern, at least for Dawn and Suzy. After a big, hearty breakfast of bacon or ham and eggs, country fries, and hot biscuits dripping with wild honey, they would stroll down to the working corrals. There they'd watch the sorting and branding, the dehorning and vaccinating of the calves that had been born during the winter. When they got tired of the dust, noise, and confusion they'd pack up a lunch in their saddlebags and take long, lovely rides, picnicking along the way. Dawn always took her sketch book, and Suzy, an avid reader, would tuck in her latest adventure story.

Much against her better judgment, Dawn found herself falling in love with the Rocking K. The kind of life one could have here away from the din, confusion and rat-race of modern existence was her ideal. So, for that matter, was its owner her ideal of the perfect man. Except for that arrogant cynicism of his! To be fair, she supposed it had been his wife who had made him cynical, but she'd bet he was *born* arrogant.

She couldn't help but be curious about his dead wife. It was unfathomable to Dawn how the woman could have been dissatisfied with a world like this, a man like Dan Kane, and a daughter who only needed a little uncritical attention to make her flower. She must have been crazy!

Impatiently, Dawn scolded herself. Dan Kane and his world—a world in which she could never be anything but a paid employee—were too much in her thoughts, and she didn't like it. Physical attraction was the first step towards love, and love in this case was spelled *Disaster* with a capital *D*. Only work provided Dawn with a haven from her muddled and pointless reflections, and on Dan's orders Sam had set up a small work area for her in a small nook of the spacious living room. There, in the evenings, she could experiment with her watercolours while Suzy read or watched television. Dan and his foreman went to bed early, usually not long after dinner. For them the days were gruelling; the backbreaking work of the roundup lasted from sunup to sundown.

The roundup finally began drawing to an end, however, and as the days grew warmer, Dan started returning early to take a swim with his daughter. Dawn always declined to join them, silently cursing herself for throwing away her old bathing suit when she packed to leave San Antonio. Thinking she might not have a suit he'd told Suzy to show her where the spares were kept for guests. But it only took one glance for Dawn to see that the ones her size were as scanty as her own. Simply imagining the bold, mocking look Dan would give her if he saw her in a revealing, sexy bikini made her blood run cold, so she always came up with one excuse or another for not swimming. She could see he believed none of them. His manner towards her since that first night had been one of disinterested friendliness, just what one would expect from a courteous employer. But there was always something unspoken in his voice, unacknowledged in his glance—an infuriating, taunting nuance of tone or posture that told her that in Dan Kane's eyes she was drab, inhibited, and silly. Sometimes there was something else in his eyes, too, something so brief and fleeting that Dawn couldn't place it—a troubled, perplexed look . . .

'Oh, come on in, Dawn,' begged Suzy. 'The water's great!'

It was late on their first really hot afternoon, and Dawn, working at a table, was watching her charge swim.

'No, I want to finish this drawing.' Dawn didn't want to admit that it was too close to the time Dan sometimes returned home. Otherwise she'd have been tempted. It would have been heavenly to be diving into that beautiful, cool, turquoise water.

Disappointed, Suzy started swimming lazy laps and Dawn returned to her work. Suddenly someone tugged playfully on her ponytail. Startled, she looked up to see Dan looming over her. It was always a disquietingly sensual sight to see him in swimming trunks. Dan's physique was superb, and he was tanned a handsome bronze. Powerful muscles rippled across his broad shoulders and down his lean torso. Adding to his virile good looks, a thick mat of dark, curly hair covered his chest.

'Why don't you ever swim? Afraid I might find out you have legs?' His sardonic blue eyes gleamed with amusement when she blushed to the roots of her hair.

'Of course not,' she sputtered, disconcerted by how close he was to the truth.

'Or perhaps bathing suits are too immodest for you. Maybe I can get Hannah to rustle up a flour sack for you to wear.'

At that moment Suzy, turning to recross the pool, saw her father and squealed in excitement. He tossed his towel over a nearby chair and dived in. Dawn couldn't help admiring his faultless dive and powerful strokes as he playfully raced his daughter across the pool. Selfconscious, unsure of herself, and quite rattled, Dawn got up to leave, but Hannah came out just then with a huge pitcher of lemonade. Suzy and Dan pulled themselves out of the pool and Dan made Hannah sit down and join them.

'I should be helping Ellen and Pat with the pies right this minute,' she fussed, sitting down while Suzy poured everyone drinks.

Ellen and Pat were cowhands' wives who worked as part-time house help. With the house-party just a few days away they were putting in extra hours helping Hannah prepare for it.

'Don't worry, I can always order some frozen ones,' Dan lightly teased the housekeeper.

Hannah bristled at the mention of convenience foods. In her world they were used only by immoral and lazy cooks. 'I'll quit first!'

Everyone laughed, including Hannah.

'By the way,' she said, after sipping some of her drink, 'did Suzy remember to mention she's grown out of her party dresses? I went through her wardrobe yesterday and she doesn't have a single dress she can still wear.'

Suzy squirmed in her chair and frowned. Dan shot her a stern glance. 'No, she didn't,' he said.

'Oh, Daddy, I hate parties! Can't I just go stay at Sam's house for the weekend?' As the foreman, Sam had a small, comfortable house of his own not far from the big one.

'No.'

Suzy's face clouded, but she knew better than to argue. That single syllable had been chiselled in granite.

'I'll fly you and Dawn into San Antonio tomorrow; there's some business that I could take care of. So you can have the whole day to shop.' He turned his head and looked at Dawn, his blue eyes mocking her. 'Unless I miss my guess, you don't have anything to wear either. Or do you want to hide at Sam's too?'

Dawn flushed a little, but she casually took a sip of lemonade. She forced a light smile. 'I might just do that.'

Suzy looked stricken, as if she had been thrown to the lions and her sole protector had defected to the Roman side. 'You wouldn't do that, would you?' she asked in wild appeal.

'Of course she wouldn't,' said Dan smoothly, 'so you'll both need to do some shopping, and that's the end of that.'

Having made an early start the next morning, they reached the shopping district on the Paseo del Rio by nine-thirty. Somehow this unplanned excursion to San Antonio highlighted to Dawn the size of the gulf between herself and her employer. She couldn't even begin to imagine what it would be like to decide to shop on the spur of the moment, with no thought of what it might cost.

What a contrast there was between Dan and her father, who hadn't set foot off their Arizona ranch a dozen times in five years. Did Dan Kane know how lucky he was to be able to afford a crew that could run the Rocking K in his absence? No, that wasn't fair, she had to admit; it was more than luck. Dan Kane knew how to pick good men and how to mould them into a top-notch, hard-working, loyal crew that would allow him to drop the reins for a day, a week, a month even, and know that the ranch would continue to run efficiently. She heard he frequently did just that, and wondered if he were the kind of man who played as hard as he worked.

As Dan pulled the rented car over to the kerb, she wondered idly where his favourite playground was—Dallas, San Francisco, New York? Abroad, perhaps? And who were his favourite playmates? Obviously, they would have to be women sophisticated enough to enjoy being wined, dined, and loved by a man who firmly had no intention of committing himself to them. Dawn tried to picture herself accepting such a relationship and couldn't. To her, the words love and commitment were synonymous.

Dan turned off the engine, pulled an envelope out of his jacket pocket, and handed it to Dawn, who was sitting in the back seat. 'Here are two letters of credit; one for Suzy and one for you.'

'But I don't—'

'Your attendance at the house-party is job-related,' he said firmly, interrupting her. 'I insist on paying for the clothes you need. Consider it a uniform allowance.' He glanced at his daughter beside him and smiled. 'Enjoy yourself, squirt, and I'll meet you two back here at four o'clock, okay?'

This time he included Dawn in his smile. He could look so devilishly charming when he felt like it, she couldn't help thinking in irritation, as she tried to ignore her thudding heart.

'Okay, Dad,' said Suzy, hopping out of the car and shutting the door behind her.

When Dawn put her hand on the back of the car seat in front of her and began to get out, Dan placed his hand deliberately on top of it. She stared up at him, startled, as he gently but firmly grasped it, stopping her.

'One more thing, Dawn,' he murmured in a tone of mock despair as his eyes flicked sardonically over her body. 'Pick out some things that fit you for once, and try to get something that doesn't look like your grandmother's old clothes.'

'Oh! You're insufferable!' she muttered, giving him what she hoped was a withering glance as she pulled her hand away and got quickly out of the car. The sound of his low laugh rang in her ears as she watched him move into the stream of traffic.

'Do you know what I'd like to do first?' she said, forcing her attention away from that incredibly infuriating man to the forlorn-looking girl at her side.

'What?' Suzy asked listlessly.

'Go into that sidewalk café over there and have a cup of hot chocolate and a piece of cake.'

Suzy's expression lightened instantly. 'Great. Maybe then we could even go to the zoo afterwards?'

Dawn laughed. 'No way, young lady. It's strictly business after our snack. Aren't you looking forward at all to buying some new clothes?'

'No,' Suzy responded grumpily as they walked towards the nearby café. 'They won't make me look any better, so why bother?'

It wasn't until they were seated and the waitress had brought their order and departed that Dawn said, 'Actually, Suzy, I was thinking last night about something that might give you a different look. You know, I don't think long hair really suits you. I bet a shorter, curly hairstyle would look really pretty on you.'

Dawn made the suggestion lightly in case the idea threatened the young girl. It was always a wrench to make a dramatic change in hairstyle, and Dawn knew Suzy's hair had never been cut.

To her surprise Suzy didn't reject the idea out of hand. The girl took a sip of hot chocolate and looked at Dawn. 'Your hair doesn't look so hot either,' she said somewhat defensively. 'It's too wavy to be pulled back into a ponytail.'

'You're absolutely right,' Dawn agreed, smiling.

Suzy looked disconcerted for a moment; she had expected Dawn to be offended. 'To tell you the truth,' she said slowly in a small voice, 'one of the reasons I liked you right away was that you looked so . . . oh, I don't know . . . homey and comfortable. Not like those glamorous fashion plates Daddy brings to the ranch sometimes. They always make me feel so uncomfortable.'

Dawn reached out and gave her hand a gentle squeeze. 'I'd be uncomfortable, too, if all I'd been exposed to were wealthy women who know what professionally styled hair, good make-up and well-designed clothes can do. They can make almost anyone look glamorous. You just haven't had a mother to teach you some of those things.'

Suzy looked at her wide-eyed, wanting to believe her. 'But if you know about those things, why do you look so plain?'

Dawn was hurt in spite of herself. Why did Suzy have to be so darned honest? 'For various reasons,' she said. 'Lack of money for one, but mainly because I'm not particularly interested in attracting men at this time in my life.'

'Oh.' Suzy digested that. 'I'd like to see what you'd look like all dressed up, anyway.'

Dawn shrugged and responded offhandedly, 'Maybe I should get my hair cut and shaped too.' As she said it she realised the idea wasn't as casual as she'd made it sound. The presumptuous and overbearing way Dan Kane treated her—especially those infuriating gibes about her looks—had roused her rebellious spirit. What if she responded to his challenge? What if she were to change from 'prim,' 'drab,' and 'uptight'—all words he had flung at her—to beautiful and alluring? Yes, and *sexy*! She'd give a lot to see the expression on his arrogant, know-it-all face. Of course she didn't care a straw about what he and his fashion-plate girl friends thought about her looks, she reassured herself stoutly. She just wanted to *show* him. She'd show Dan Kane that she wasn't afraid of him, or of any other man for that matter.

No longer was she a timid seventeen-year-old incapable of putting a man in his place if he tried overstepping himself. But he could keep his 'uniform allowance'. She'd buy her clothes with the money she'd earned. Even if she spent half of it she'd still have enough money to repay her father.

Dawn finished her coffee and put her cup down. 'Shall I call up some beauty parlours and find one that will take us both without a reservation?'

'All right.' Suzy smiled—a little shyly, a little excitedly. 'I think I'd like that.'

The second shop Dawn called was able to take them right away. She was impressed with the looks of the women in the shop, and confidently put Suzy into the hands of one of the stylists. To her own stylist, an elegant and flawlessly groomed woman in her fifties, she said that although she wanted a good shaping, she'd prefer her hair to be at least shoulder-length.

'That's just what I would have suggested,' said the stylist after she had brushed Dawn's hair. 'You have such thick, healthy hair. If you took too much weight off, it would curl rather than wave. But let's try a little layering.'

With her head tilted to one side the woman looked at her, nodded her approval of what she saw, and got to work.

Two hours later when they left the shop, Dawn had trouble getting Suzy to take more than three consecutive steps without stopping to goggle at her appearance in the reflection from a store window. She really couldn't blame her; even Dawn had been startled by the change in Suzy's appearance. Her hair had been completely layered, from the soft bangs to just a few inches above her collar. A permanent had turned her limp hair into a rich brown riot of pliant curls which filled out her narrow face and softened the angular line of her jaw. It made her look incredibly prettier and more lively; she was almost unrecognisable.

When Suzy wasn't looking at herself she was casting adoring eyes at Dawn's lovely hair, and Dawn had a hard time stopping herself from doing the same thing. Tawny and full-bodied, it swung sensually against her cheeks in the most delightful way.

Stopping only briefly for lunch, they spent most of their time shopping for clothes, and then bought some make-up for Dawn. After Suzy heatedly pointed out that she was almost fourteen, Dawn allowed herself to be talked into letting her charge buy a pale pink lipstick. It was a delight to see the girl's confidence growing by the minute. She was even walking straighter and holding her shoulders back.

'Do you mind if I take some time to shop for presents for my family, Suzy?'

'Uh-uh. I wish I had brothers and sisters,' Suzy said enviously, then added, 'If there's any of my money left, I'd like to buy something for my dad, Sam, and Hannah.'

By the time the gift shopping was done, and a package mailed to Dawn's family along with a money order to her father, they were both exhausted.

Just before Dan picked them up, Dawn found a rubber band in her pocket and pulled her hair back into a ponytail. She explained to Suzy that it would be more fun to look pretty all at once, with her new clothes and makeup on as well. The uneasy truth was that she was getting cold feet. But all she needed was a little more time, she maintained to herself, while trying to calm the sudden racing of her heart.

As if on cue, the car came into view and pulled alongside the curb in front of them. Dan's first glance was for his daughter, and he was gratifyingly effusive in his praise.

'You look *wonderful*, honey! For a minute I thought Dawn had traded my little girl in for another one. What did she do—pay a good fairy to wave a wand over you?'

'Oh, *Daddy*!' Suzy giggled, flowering visibly in the glow of her father's admiration.

The look he gave to Dawn was very different. Behind

the usual thinly veiled disdain his eyes glittered with smouldering anger. It wasn't hard to figure out why. She was still her frumpy self, and inasmuch as she had handed him back an uncashed letter of credit he had of course assumed that all the packages were Suzy's. As she got into the car she had to work to keep from smiling. Poor baby, she thought sarcastically, he's so used to seeing people jump when he gives an order, it must be a novel experience when someone defies him.

Of course, she amended ruefully, she actually *had* jumped, hadn't she? Half those packages were hers, but at least she could decide when and if she'd let him know that. Meanwhile, he could just go ahead and stew!

But they weren't back at the Rocking K two minutes before Dan Kane sent Suzy off to put away her new clothes and demanded Dawn's presence in his study.

'I think we ought to get one thing straight right now,' he said in a granite tone which went very well with his black scowl. 'I told you to get some decent clothes, and when I give an employee an order, I expect it to be followed to the letter. Understand?'

'Perfectly,' Dawn returned crisply, glad that his insufferably arrogant tone had aroused her temper; otherwise, she'd have been quaking in her shoes before his anger. He stood there towering menacingly over her, hands jammed on narrow hips—a perfect picture of an enraged autocrat—and she suspected few people could stand up to him in this mood.

'But you're forgetting one thing, Mr Kane, I'm your employee only under duress, remember?' Her eyes sparkled with temper. 'You're free to fire me any time you so desire, and *nothing* could make me happier!'

She had him over a barrel, but she wasn't foolish enough to gloat as she watched him digest her words.

The look in his eyes went from flaming anger to grim displeasure as the two of them stood there glaring at each other.

'If it weren't for Suzy, I'd do just that,' he muttered scathingly, 'because you are by far the most *exasperating*, *stubborn*, *mule-headed* female I've ever had the misfortune to stumble across.'

Except for the 'female', Dawn thought agitatedly, those words described Dan Kane to a T. And it would be easy to add a few more, but they wouldn't be ladylike.

'Well, as long as you have stumbled across me,' she said as glacially as she could, 'you'd better understand that *I* decide how I look and what I wear. And what I think,' she added recklessly, drawing courage from she didn't know where.

'Is that a fact, now?' he drawled, suddenly giving her a taunting smile that unnerved her in a way his anger hadn't.

'Yes,' she declared, flushing, furious at herself for throwing out what had amounted to a challenge. 'That's a fact. Will that be all?' She gripped the back of a chair so that he wouldn't see that she was trembling.

'Yes,' he said slowly, while his eyes glided sardonically over her. 'For now.'

Over the next few days, Dan's anger cooled, but he goaded her unmercifully whenever Suzy wasn't around.

'You're so damn inhibited maybe I should have offered you a year's worth of free visits to a psychiatrist instead of art school tuition,' he taunted on the morning the guests were to arrive, when he saw her wearing her usual old clothes and hairstyle.

What made it especially upsetting was the fact that Dawn was beginning to agree with him. Despite her brave thoughts during the shopping trip, her stomach churned just *thinking* about emerging from the refuge she had created for herself so long ago. She really had meant to wear her new tight-fitting whipcord jeans and matching cowgirl shirt that morning, but hadn't come up with the courage.

And now even Suzy was looking puzzled. Dawn feared that any minute the child might blurt out to her father that Dawn, too, had purchased some new clothes for the party. Fortunately, the distant buzz of an airplane engine heralded the arrival of the first guest and Dawn was able to fade into the background.

The drone of planes flying in and landing on the ranch airstrip continued through the morning and early afternoon. Occasionally the drone became a whoosh as guests plummeted down in sleek private jets. Soon the area around the landing strip took on the look of a small airport, and Dawn shook her head in amazement. The fabled wealth of the Texas oil men was not all fable. The women were jewelled and fashionably encased in Parisian or New York designer outfits, or in elaborate silver- or gold-fringed cowgirl outfits. The men were a more motley assortment. Some were suave playboys who looked as if they'd jetted directly from the Riviera, while others were weather-beaten old codgers who dressed as if they didn't have five cents to their name. They all had one thing in common, though: the serene and unmistakable self-confidence of the very rich.

Ironically, it wasn't a caustic remark of Dan's that finally spurred Dawn to action, but an overheard remark by his date for the weekend. Meg Bronson was a stunning red-head with gorgeous green eyes who had spent the whole morning hanging all over him, a sight that irked Dawn tremendously—if irrationally—all the more because he seemed to be enjoying the woman's disgustingly possessive manner.

A casual question about her to Suzy elicited a wrinkled nose followed by a flood of information, most of it subjective in the extreme. Meg Bronson was from a frightfully rich family, she had been trying to snare Dan Kane for two years with no success, she was boring, and she was a snob.

The last point, at least, was quickly verified when Dan introduced Dawn as Suzy's companion for the summer. Meg literally looked down her nose at Dawn, murmured 'How do you do,' with all the warmth she might have used to address a toad, and tugged on Dan's arm to end the brief exchange and drag him away before Dawn could even reply.

That was extremely unpleasant, but not the worst of it. When they were no more than ten or fifteen feet away, the woman's seductive laugh floated back. 'Why didn't you tell me, darling,' she said, and Dawn saw her squeeze Dan's arm, 'that there wasn't anything to be jealous *about*?'

Dawn had little doubt that Meg had meant to be overheard. She was jealous, all right. Perhaps not of Dawn herself, but certainly of her full-time presence on the Rocking K. To a woman like Meg every woman was a potential enemy to be cut down to size as quickly as possible.

When a general swim time was announced, and Dawn, like everyone else, retreated to change into a bathing suit, she strode to her room with grim determination.

She pulled the rubber band from her hair and leaned over to brush it from the nape of the neck down. Stroking vigorously, she managed to calm her nerves.

Then she straightened and brushed it back in the other direction. The honey colour gleamed with russet highlights as it swung to her shoulders, the ends curling under softly.

A touch of eyeshadow set off her luminous, golden-brown eyes to mysterious perfection, and glossy peach-coloured lipstick made her lips full and astonishingly sensual. Dawn stood staring at her reflection, lost in thought for a long time. Like Suzy, she was barely recognisable.

Her bathing suit was a bit scantier than she remembered, but there was no question that it showed off her full, shapely breasts and long slender legs. It didn't exactly hide the provocative swell of her hips, either.

Dawn smiled nervously at her image. She was certainly all grown up; no doubt about that. She slipped on her new coverup and high-heeled sandals and looked again. More proper, certainly, but they gave her a sleek and stylish look which by no means distracted attention from her smoothly curving calves or the trim line of her ankles.

The pool area was alive with people laughing, swimming and lounging contentedly about when Dawn arrived. Dan Kane, in dark swimming trucks, was over by the built-in brick barbecue, where mesquite wood was being readied. His broad back to her, he was making himself and a couple of other men some drinks. His skin gleamed in the afternoon sun, and the reflected light from the pool played on his powerful muscles. As her eyes flickered over his lean, formidable body, she fought back a sudden tide of panic.

Shoring up her courage, she halted briefly near a lounge chair and took in the scene. She was pleased to see Suzy, in a bathing suit, sitting on the side of the pool with her feet in the water, comfortably chatting with two girls her own age. At the sight of Dawn, she grinned. Several other people saw the striking-looking girl with the honey-brown hair too. Casually, as if she weren't aware of the eyes on her, Dawn opened her coverup and shrugged it off. Dan noted the sudden hiatus in conversation around him as his companions caught sight of Dawn's lovely figure. In the process of taking a swallow of his drink he turned offhandedly to see who was getting all the attention.

To her secret amusement she saw him choke on the liquid in his mouth and turn red. When he started coughing, one of his friends, laughing boisterously, started pounding him on the back while another rescued his drink. Dawn was too far away to hear what Dan said when he could finally speak again, but she was sure it was a curse. She pretended not to see the ferocious scowl he gave her or the fierce lines of his angry face.

Sitting down nonchalantly, Dawn stretched out her long legs on the lounge chair and slipped on some lightly-tinted sunglasses. Although she knew she was managing to appear composed on the surface, she welcomed the protection they gave her eyes against Dan Kane's fiery gaze. She couldn't decide if he looked more like a hawk that had just discovered a viper in its nest or an enraged bull that had spotted an intruder on his territory. Either way, there was no question about whether or not she had caught his attention.

# CHAPTER FOUR

MANY of the women were wearing bikinis, and Dawn noted with relief that others were even more revealing than hers. Meg Bronson, near the cooking fires with Dan and his friends, had on a suit that was downright minuscule: three tiny patches of cobalt blue held together by ties.

'Dawn, you look super!' squealed Suzy, running up to her. 'Daddy thought so too; I could tell, even if he has been looking at you sort of funny.' She didn't pause long enough to let Dawn get in a word as she excitedly introduced the two girls with whom she'd been chatting. 'This is Terrie and Karen.'

'Hi there, Terrie and Karen,' Dawn said, smiling warmly. 'How's the water?'

'Great,' exclaimed Karen, a plump girl who looked about twelve. 'We were just going to play some water soccer. Want to play?'

'Sure,' Dawn agreed instantly. 'It'll be nice to cool off.' Whether it was the heat of the sun or the smouldering glances Dan Kane continued to shoot in her direction that made her feel warm, Dawn didn't know, but the turquoise-coloured water was an irresistible vision of coolness.

It wasn't long before several others joined the impromptu game. As far as Dawn could tell their attitude towards her was openly friendly, even though they knew she was Suzy's companion. Several of the unattached men made no secret of their admiration, but, remarkably enough, Dawn was unthreatened by it. She lost track of time as the game progressed with much laughter, splashing and raillery. Several times, though, she bobbed to the surface and opened her eyes to find herself fixed by Dan's lancing gaze.

Neither he nor Meg elected to play. With every strand of her beautiful hair in place, Meg looked too incredibly sophisticated to join a rowdy game. She might, after all, get her hair wet, thought Dawn uncharitably, catching a blatantly hostile glance from the woman. To be honest, Dawn added to herself, she too might worry about such things if she didn't have naturally curly hair which was attractive wet as well as dry.

How odd it was to be thinking such things. What she didn't realise, or at least didn't admit to herself, was that the agitation stimulated by Dan Kane's awareness of her had sparked a long-slumbering vivacity, adding to her looks and confidence both. Some of the old sombreness seemed to be melting away as she swam, laughed, or screamed when one of the young men ducked her by surprise. She felt as exquisitely alive as if she'd just emerged from a cocoon.

Heavenly aromas of sizzling steaks, ribs, and chicken filled the air, finally enticing the swimmers from the water. The exercise had heightened appetites, and soon the crowd had made sizable incursions into the sumptuous piles of barbecued meats, ranch-style beans, potato salad, roasted corn-on-the-cob, and sourdough biscuits. Hannah's famous pecan and apple pie followed with gallons of rich, strong coffee.

After the prolonged picnic-style dinner, when a cool, early-evening breeze wafted through the courtyard, the swimmers dispersed to change into dry clothes. Dawn shooed Suzy and her newly discovered friends off to change and was passing by the small study off the atrium when Dan walked into the corridor. His firm stride told her trouble was coming.

'May I talk to you for a moment?' he asked crisply. It was a command, not a question.

'Of course.' She pretended a mild bewilderment, but she didn't have to feign the touch of fear that sprang to life as she stared up at the grim set to the lines of his face. Unlike the last time she had summarily been hauled into the lion's den, she didn't feel confident about the outcome of this battle. Nor did she know exactly how she wanted it to end. Would she be relieved if he fired her and she never saw him again? Or was she just kidding herself? Dan's blue eyes were icy as he steered her into the room and shut the door.

'What a low-down, mean, *contemptible* trick you just played,' he grated, his anger radiating from him as he paced the small room.

'Trick? I don't understand,' she responded in confusion. To Dawn's surprise her voice was steady despite the butterflies in her stomach set off by his angry baritone and scowling countenance. 'You've been badgering me to come out of my shell, as you call it, for weeks! Would you rather I wore one of Hannah's flour sacks after all?'

'Don't play the wide-eyed innocent,' he drawled sarcastically, stopping in front of her with a chilling look. 'You didn't get to the age of twenty-three without finding out before this that you have a figure like a damn Playboy bunny!'

'I don't think my measurements are any concern of yours. And I don't recall your inquiring about them in our employment discussions.' Her luminous eyes flashed at the injustice of it all. The nerve of the man! Taunting her because she hadn't done anything with her looks, and then giving her hell when she finally *did*!

'I'm not referring to your metamorphosis into a sex goddess. I knew you had potential . . .' His gaze momentarily dropped to the floor. 'Perhaps I wasn't aware of quite how much,' he muttered grimly. His eyes came up again, hot and ominous, and his voice rose. 'But that's beside the point,' he raged. 'I'm referring to your timing, and you know it!'

An angry flush spread over her cheeks as she stood speechless in the face of his blazing fury.

'Oh, it was great fun to be right in the middle of telling my friends about my daughter's competent but spinsterish companion, and then—right *then*!—you walk out practically naked, looking like a . . . !'

Dawn's cheeks grew even hotter as she finally understood the position she had naïvely placed him in. 'I certainly didn't intend—'

'And since then,' he went on, ignoring her, 'I must have taken twenty sly pokes in the ribs. Just who was I trying to kid about whose companion you were? The implication being, in case you're dense,' he said, enunciating his words as if he were speaking to an idiot, 'that you're *my* playmate!' He took a step closer to her.

No wonder he was so angry. 'I didn't mean . . . I mean, I didn't think . . .' Her voice trailed off. He was so close to her now that she felt a great deal more than fear; a strange and thrilling excitement coursed lushly through her veins. She compelled her legs, suddenly trembling and weak, to step back.

'You didn't think,' he murmured grimly. 'Well, I don't believe you. How long have you been planning this big butterfly scene? Ever since you discovered how much money I have?'

The ugly accusation hit her like a slap in the face. Her anger flared, igniting glints of amber in her eyes and stiffening her spine.

'Sorry to be the one to put a dent in that colossal ego of yours, Mr Kane,' she retorted coldly, 'but there are women, myself included, who don't spend all their time scheming to catch you! I may have been angry at your constant badgering, and I may have been annoyed at your snob of a lady friend for deliberately snubbing me, and I may have picked a poor time to lash out—'

He laughed shortly, but the strong line of his jaw didn't relax.

'—but that's all.' Although some instinct warned her to bite back the words welling up inside her, she didn't heed it. 'As for the other, I wouldn't want you if you *were* served on a million-dollar platter!' She flung the words at him.

'You're very good at throwing out challenges, Dawn Richards,' he said in a smooth, strangely ominous tone. 'I wonder how well you'd respond if I took you up on one.' His eyes roved brazenly over her in lordly inspection, raking her body under the scanty coverup and lingering on her long, slender legs. He might have been an eastern potentate assessing a slave on an auction block, and she might have been . . . It didn't bear thinking about.

'It wasn't meant as a challenge,' she countered angrily.

Simmering, she stood there trying not to flinch under his gaze. Unfortunately, she was ridiculously susceptible to the striking good looks and undeniable sexual magnetism of the man, and it put her at a considerable disadvantage. His open-throated shirt, donned against the cooling evening air, was the same blue shade as his eyes, and it set off his dark hair and bronzed skin. And what was worse—much worse—she knew instinctively that he too was aware of his effect on her, regardless of what she might say.

Abruptly his expression changed, and he ran a hand through his hair. 'I should have my head examined, but I believe you didn't plan this.'

Dawn dropped her eyes to hide the relief that flowed through her.

'I've had a hellish afternoon,' he grumbled, briefly glowering at her again. 'If just one more "friend" comments about the Rocking K's distracting new scenery I'm going to throw the lot of them out. I mean it!'

'I'm sorry,' she murmured contritely, then added, 'Look, Dan, this whole situation just isn't working out. We seem to rub each other the wrong way. Maybe it would really be better all around if I quit.'

Anger flared in his eyes again. 'Don't talk nonsense. Although I can't say I have a terribly high opinion of your brains right now, even you must realise Suzy's absolutely blossoming under your care. I can't remember the last time she enjoyed herself so much, and I know I've never seen her relate to girls her own age before.'

The combination insult-compliment flustered her for a moment, and then suddenly all she wanted was to flee from his unnerving and overpowering presence. She turned to go. 'Then perhaps I'll retire for the evening—'

'Absolutely not,' he said, grasping her arm. His hand was warm on her cool flesh. Then he added wryly, 'I'd have to spend half the evening fending off inquiries from that circle of breathless admirers you gathered around yourself so quickly. You've caused enough trouble today; spare me that.' He spun on his heel and walked from the room.

He had been right about a circle of admirers. It was two in the morning before Dawn decided to call it a night. Although a few people had retired earlier—Dawn made sure Suzy was among them—most had stayed on to gossip, to dance, or to play cards. And Dawn, in her new sunflower-yellow dress with its flattering halter top, had received more than her share of male attention. Sleepy and tired she may have been as she headed back to her room, but she'd had a fantastic evening.

Although she had never once lacked for young dancing partners, she had also spent time with some of the older guests. Somehow the word had got out about Great-great-uncle Jack dying at the Alamo, and the old-timers treated Dawn like a long-lost relative, especially after she had truthfully told them she enjoyed nothing more than hearing about the old days.

There was one older guest, Duke Austin, that she particularly wished someone would introduce her to, after hearing he was a major collector of American art and quite an authority on contemporary Western artists, many of whom he knew personally. How exciting it would be to talk to someone like that! She wondered if she might walk up and introduce herself; he certainly didn't look intimidating. In fact, with his wiry frame and legs bowed from years in the saddle, he reminded her strongly of her grandfather. But she hung back, uneasy at intruding on him.

Dawn didn't realise she had been standing hesitantly on the edge of the crowd and looking in Austin's direction until she felt a strong hand on her elbow. She looked up into Dan Kane's mocking blue eyes, and her heart lurched at the sight of him, so that she had to make a conscious effort to retain her poise. Darn him! During the evening, whenever she caught him looking at her—not that it happened often—she became more and more conscious of his effect on her. It really wasn't fair, especially when she so desperately wished she could be indifferent to him.

'Haven't you learned yet that standing around shilly-shallying doesn't get you anywhere?' he murmured, guiding her firmly in Duke Austin's direction.

'Yes, but I couldn't . . . I mean I didn't want to—' She stopped abruptly as Austin, seeing them heading in his direction, excused himself from a cluster of people and came to join them.

'So this is the little gal who's doing such a good job bringing little Suzy out of her shell,' the old man drawled with a sharp Texas twang, smiling warmly at Dawn. 'I wouldn't have recognised the child if not for that stubborn Kane jaw.'

'There's not much Dawn can do about that, I'm afraid,' Dan said with a wry smile. 'But I agree, Dawn's certainly worked wonders. Dawn, this is a good friend, Duke Austin, our neighbour to the west.'

Confused by Dan's generous compliment and cordiality, Dawn smiled uncertainly and extended her hand.

Austin gave it a hearty shake. 'Sorry my wife couldn't be here tonight—she'll be tickled pink when she hears about Suzy and about you.' He glanced at Dan. 'You all will have to come to dinner soon.'

'Name the date. I'll be going up to summer pasture for a few weeks, but any time after that is fine. By the way,' Dan added casually, 'there's another reason why I thought you might want to meet Dawn. She does some pretty impressive artwork with Western themes. I think you'd enjoy seeing it. Pardon me,' he then said smooth-ly. 'I see someone I need to talk to.' And he was gone.

Taken completely by surprise, Dawn protested weakly. 'Dan's exaggerating, Mr Austin. I've only been working a few years, and I haven't had any training yet.'

Austin brushed her comment aside with a snort. 'First, call me Duke. And second, I don't hold with these fancy art schools. They try to turn everyone into a danged abstract expressionist. Or worse.'

The face he made when he said 'abstract', made Dawn bite her lip to keep from laughing. Clearly Duke Austin was no lover of modern art. But then neither was she.

'As Dan knows, I'd sooner look at art than stand around jawing,' Austin said stoutly, 'so let's go have a look at your work. No time like the present.'

Dawn had shown her work only to a few family members and close friends. They all thought she was quite talented, but of course their judgment was more than a little subjective. So it was with nervous hands that she pulled some of her drawings out of the folder to show them to her first unbiased and knowledgeable viewer.

It pleased her to see Duke's slow and careful perusal. When he finally looked up he shook his head violently, and for a second Dawn's heart plummeted.

'Art school would be a waste of time for you,' he said stoutly. 'What you need to do is to take a few lessons from a top-notch Western artist. Somebody like Buck Harvey. He could show you a few things to add some polish—not that you need much—without fooling around with your style.'

Yes, thought Dawn, and if horses had wings and I were a millionaire like everyone else here, I'd just go look up Buck Harvey. The idea of somebody like her approaching so well-known an artist was preposterous.

Nevertheless, she glowed with pleasure at Duke's kindly words. The idea that someone thought she had already developed her own personal style was thrilling.

He didn't wait for her reply. 'I'd like to take a couple of these to show a friend, if you don't mind. I'll take good care of 'em.' At her shy assent, he picked out her drawing of Dan in the Alamo courtyard and one of Sam giving Paint his evening cube of sugar.

The rest of the night was spent dancing and talking with a variety of interesting, unattached males, and to her surprise she found it relatively easy to deflect the kind of attention she didn't want. Those years of handling five active and rebellious brothers and sisters, and dealing with the household responsibilities as well, had built her confidence and self-reliance without her knowing it.

As she finally walked to her room, though, it was Dan she found herself thinking about. Not once had he asked her to dance. She tried to analyse her feelings about that and had to admit that, absurd as it was, what she was feeling was disappointment. It would have been nice to have had the chance to thank him properly for introducing her to Duke. That *was* the reason, she told herself, that she was disappointed. It certainly wasn't because he was the most attractive, magnetic man there. Not at all, she maintained stoutly, if not convincingly.

One thing she did admit to herself was that she actually owed him a lot. He had done for her what he said *she*'d done for Suzy. He had shaken her out of her shell. She had never felt so totally alive—alive but sleepy, she amended, stifling a yawn. And she could hug herself every time she remembered what Duke Austin had said about her drawings.

Once in her room she was sure she could sleep for a

week. Wearily, she slipped into a nightgown and bent to turn back the bedcovers. She heard a soft rustling noise just beneath her hand, and the whispery sound set off a wave of fear that quickly turned to terror when the glistening snake suddenly darted from under the sheet.

Instinctively Dawn screamed. The snake seemed even more panicked than she was, but it veered horribly towards her, and she couldn't help screaming again.

The door seemed to explode inward and Dan's tall frame filled it. Taking in the harmless snake and Dawn's undressed state in a single glance, he turned back to the corridor, continuing to block the view into the room with his body. The hallway was filled with the sound of running footsteps.

'It's nothing, Lew. A harmless snake. I'll take care of it. Tell the others to go to bed.' He closed the door.

Rooted to the spot, Dawn could only watch as Dan easily caught the writhing creature, opened the sliding glass door, and tossed it out.

'Women!' he said in exasperation as he turned back to her.

An immense wave of relief flooded through her, but with it came the excruciating realisation that she had practically nothing on. Only her tissue-thin nightgown stood between her and Dan's mocking but definitely hungry eyes. He laughed as she turned several shades of pink and grabbed the Mexican blanket from her bed to cover herself. Then he lifted his eyes to her face.

'That poor snake wouldn't hurt a fly,' he said, chuckling. 'Well, maybe a fly, but I assure you, pretty young women aren't on its menu.'

'I'm sorry. I couldn't help it.' She was still shuddering at the memory of the wriggling body. 'My brothers put a snake in my apron pocket once,' she said, her voice shaking. 'I reached in to get a handkerchief and . . .' Her shoulders crawled with a convulsive little shudder.

'Don't worry about this happening again. I know a certain kid around here who isn't going to sit for a week. Hey, you're still shaking,' Dan added, his voice gentle with sudden concern. He reached out and gathered her into his strong arms. 'Your skin is like ice,' he said, and she felt his warm, big hands on her back.

Never in Dawn's life—except perhaps as a child in her parents' arms—had she found herself feeling so instantly safe and protected. Her fear melted away as he held her close against his warm, strong chest, while gently, so very gently stroking her back. The blissful sensation of drawing on his strength, of depending on his calm, sure power while cradled in his arms was so indescribably wonderful, she wished only to stay there forever without moving.

But belatedly her common sense began asserting itself. What must he be thinking! She started to pull away, her face averted so that he couldn't see her heightened colour. 'I'm sorry,' she murmured, 'I've tried everything to cure myself of my fear of snakes, but nothing's worked.'

'No need to apologise,' Dan said quietly, loosening his arms a little. 'In fact'—and Dawn could tell he was smiling—'I have to admit I've been enjoying myself.' He tilted her chin up so he could look into her face. 'Feeling better? How about some brandy?'

She shook her head, not trusting herself to speak. Her breathing was becoming slightly ragged as she became more and more conscious of sensations that had nothing to do with her fear of snakes or the novelty of being in a safe haven. In fact, she began to feel distinctly *unsafe*— vulnerable not only to Dan but to emotions stirring unbidden inside herself as she stared up into those gentle blue eyes a few inches from her own. Dawn barely dared to breathe, lest she give herself away. But it was no use. Her golden-brown eyes mirrored her thoughts and betrayed her.

Dan's eyes clouded as he looked deeply into her own. 'You look like you're fine now. In fact, too fine . . . and too beautiful.' The tips of his fingers travelled lingeringly from her chin to her hair. Slowly he entwined them into the soft thickness of the tresses. She was transfixed, aware of an exquisite excitement that had replaced those nebulous stirrings of a moment ago.

'You could drive any man insane,' he said in a low, silky voice that sent shivers down her spine. Astonishingly, his mouth came down on hers.

Trembling under the heated pressure of his lips, Dawn resisted for a moment, but his embrace only tightened. She had let go of the blanket to push him away and now she felt it slip so that her breasts were against his broad chest. She could feel the heavy thud of his heart beating under her palms. Then, dissolving under the fiery persuasion of his mouth, she lost the ability to think. Trembling, her lips parted at his fierce insistence. Her breath quickened as she found her arms around his neck and her body arched against his. She seemed to be floating, spinning . . .

An automatic warning signal went off in her mind, bringing her back to reality, as she felt one of his hands, trailing fire, move down the V-shaped neckline of her gown and slide caressingly beneath the material. Marshalling her thoughts with difficulty, she tried to put from her mind the shaft of sheer pleasure that shot through her. Things were getting out of hand. She needed to concentrate.

'No, please don't,' she cried huskily, finally breaking away from his kiss. His embrace slackened as if he, too, suddenly sensed danger.

His blue eyes seemed almost to soften for a moment, but then he lifted his shoulders in a shrug. His voice turned harsh and his visage darkened. 'The scenery is too goddamn distracting around the Rocking K these days.' Abruptly he let her go and strode out of the room, banging the door behind him.

Her mind was in turmoil, and for a few moments she simply stood there with her eyes closed, letting the strength flow back into her unsteady legs, and waiting for her shallow breath to return to something like normal. Hardly caring if there might be another snake—or a dozen for that matter—Dawn climbed in between the sheets and pulled the covers up to her chin. Although her body slowly began to cool and relax her thoughts continued to race. It wasn't just the kiss. She could hardly blame Dan for taking advantage of the situation. What red-blooded American male wouldn't? It was more her response. To her shock and dismay she had briefly responded with total abandon in Dan's arms. What must he think of her? Passion had hit her like an avalanche and now that he was gone she felt mortified; weak and drained.

Far worse, infinitely worse, was the worrisome knowledge that she was more than half-way in love with him. She'd been able to resist him while he had shown only his arrogant, egoistic self. But the house party had revealed a whole new side of him. He had been generous, kind, considerate, and hospitable—to an employee, no less, and a troublesome one at that! And just now he had been so wonderfully tender and comforting—at least until she'd stared up at him like a lovesick calf, probably begging to be kissed.

So many of his qualities were ones she longed for in a man. And to find them in a man who was the physical embodiment of her ideal of the heroic, romantic West was like a dream. A deadly dream, she thought leadenly. It wouldn't be so bad if she were willing to settle for a brief affair—or even a long one. He was physically attracted to her, she certainly couldn't deny that any longer, and no doubt he would be quite accommodating in that direction should she ever indicate interest. But she wouldn't, not with him, or with any man. Her values were as old-fashioned as the art she loved. She felt about casual liaisons, where two people made love without commitment, as she did about canvases splattered with coffee grounds and jelly, or sculptures fashioned out of rusty automobile parts. They might appeal to others but not to her.

There was only one thing for her to do. Somehow, she had to stifle her emotions before she irretrievably lost her heart to him. It wasn't going to be easy. She'd have to struggle through eight more weeks; she had a commitment to Suzy, and she wasn't going to break it. But once back in San Antonio she would be able to immerse herself in school and work, perhaps start to date, and begin to forget. Time did heal wounds. It was a cliché, but one she'd already discovered was true.

If Dawn could have found an excuse to stay in her room the next morning she would have. It wasn't only because of the embarrassment of facing Dan or because she had to put her new resolution to the test. She also dreaded people's questions about that stupid snake. Her screams had been loud enough to wake the dead, Dawn thought mournfully as she dressed, worthy of at least a copperhead or rattlesnake.

She was barely dressed when Suzy and her two friends Terrie and Karen burst in, giggling, after a quick knock.

'Morning, Dawn. Boy, you should have been up earlier! We found Ted hiding in the barn. He spent the whole night sleeping in the hayrack,' said Suzy, flopping backwards onto the bed while the other two girls draped themselves over the chairs. Teenagers never just sat, Dawn reflected, amused.

'After those fabulous screams of yours he was afraid for his life,' Terrie piped up.

'Well, I don't have the slightest sympathy for him,' Dawn said, picking up a brush and beginning to stroke her hair. 'He deserves whatever he's going to get.'

'Oh, he already got it,' giggled Karen. 'We talked him into giving himself up to his dad before Sam caught him.'

All three of the girls fell into gales of laughter.

'He chose the switch rather than the waterhole,' Terrie finally gasped after she had caught her breath. 'He's crazy about his new boots, and he was afraid the mud would ruin them.'

Dawn laughed. 'What are you girls up to this morning?' she asked, marvelling at Suzy's ease with the other two girls. Although Karen Robinson, a plump little butterball, was unthreatening, fourteen-year-old, dark-haired Terrie Haagson was as beautiful as a young colt—just the sort of girl Suzy would have called a stuck-up swan. But then Suzy herself, with her soft curls and new pale-blue denim jeans with their matching cowgirl shirt, looked rather swanlike now.

Dawn, too, was wearing a new casual but elegant Western outfit she had purchased for the house party. The tight-fitting, russet whipcord jeans emphasised her svelte, long-legged look, and the Western shirt was equally flattering. Also russet, its yoke and cuffs were in a contrasting cream-coloured material. A matching chiffon kerchief tied around her neck and knotted at the side completed the outfit. She was hoping that if she showed a brave front to Dan Kane he wouldn't guess how very much afraid and susceptible to him she was. That was something he'd grasp in a second if she retreated back into her shell.

'We want to go riding!' the girls chorused, breaking into her thoughts. 'Will you take us?'

'Sure,' Dawn responded, with a smile. 'As soon as I've had some breakfast.'

Hannah, with the catering staff flown in from San Antonio, had set up a help-yourself breakfast buffet on the long wooden dining-room table. Melons and fruits, sweet, fragrant breads of banana, date, and squash, and jams and jellies were prettily arrayed. Large silver serving pots on a sideboard contained coffee, tea, and sweet Mexican hot chocolate. Several people were still eating, sitting around the tables near the pool.

Although Suzy, Terrie, and Karen had had breakfast an hour before, they were, like all teenagers, ready to eat at any opportunity.

As expected, Dawn found herself the centre of a somewhat teasing attention, but it was a friendly, gentle bantering that surprisingly made her feel one of them. Dan was absent and Meg Bronson pointedly didn't join in. Dawn wondered if she had kept track of the time Dan had spent in Dawn's room or if Dan had emerged with a trace of lipstick on him. Something had certainly put those daggers in Meg's eyes.

Dawn and the three girls responded to Duke Austin's waved invitation to join him with their breakfasts.

'With lungs like yours, Dawn,' he said, his brown old

face creased with a grin from ear to ear, 'you can always take up opera singing if you get tired of art.'

Before Dawn had a chance to reply, Dan entered the courtyard and strode up to their table. Her heart raced so wildly at the sight of him that she was petrified at the thought the others could hear it. Fortunately, no one seemed to notice.

'Morning, kids, Duke,' he said, tipping his hat. With the Stetson shading his eyes from the sun, Dawn wasn't able to see his expression clearly enough to guess what he might be thinking. He turned slightly towards her. 'Morning, Dawn,' he said mildly. He looked at her for what seemed a long time. 'No ill effects from last night?' he drawled, with studied casualness. 'Must have been a pretty overwhelming experience.'

Unwilling to trust her voice, she shook her head, feeling herself blush under his gaze. She could see, from the way his eyes slid appreciatively over her, that he liked her new outfit. Unfortunately, she couldn't help remembering what she'd been wearing—or rather, not wearing—when he'd last seen her. The colour in her cheeks deepened further. To her relief, Suzy changed the subject.

'Dawn's going to take us riding after breakfast, Daddy.'

'Well, enjoy yourself, but be sure to ride to the south. A bunch of us are going game-bird shooting up around Black Horse Canyon.'

While Karen and Terrie selected the horses they were going to ride, Suzy saddled Tandy. Dawn, however, was disappointed to find that Paint had been taken out that morning by Sam on the cattle drive to the summer range. Indifferently, she chose another horse. She hadn't realised how much she'd become attached to Paint, and it wasn't quite the same as she swung up into the saddle. The ride was pleasant, though, and soothing to her troubled thoughts. Obediently they rode towards the hills to the south, alternately cantering and walking the horses.

When they returned to the barn in the afternoon, Dawn was waylaid by a very abject-looking eleven-year-old, walking a bit gingerly.

'I didn't know you were *really* afraid of snakes, Miss Richards,' Ted apologised, 'or I'd never have put that snake in your bed, *honest*! And I'll never do that again,' the little body said, with transparent sincerity.

'To anyone?' Dawn asked solemnly, holding back a smile. 'Because you might make someone who was never afraid of snakes before, actually become afraid.'

'To anyone, ever, I *promise*.'

Ted, his spirits revived with her forgiveness, helped Dawn and the girls curry their horses, and by the time they returned to the house for a swim, the hunters were long back after a successful morning. The party was lively that evening, and everyone dined royally on spit-roasted quail, partridge, and wild turkey served with plum and cranberry preserve.

After dinner, when people began to move about, Dawn fled every time Dan stepped in her direction. Which was not often, thanks to Meg Bronson's sharp eyes and clutching talons. Today, though, she was grateful for Meg's possessive manner, and found herself hoping wistfully that Dan would invite the woman to spend the rest of the summer. Dawn would put up with anything or anyone who could shield her from Dan Kane. Unfortunately, it wasn't long before she almost ran right into him by accident in the dimly-lit atrium, and when she did, his smile was predictably sardonic and his blue eyes mocking.

'Steady there,' he said, preventing a collision by lightly touching her arm.

'Sorry, I wasn't looking where I was going,' she apologised, giving him a shaky, noncommittal smile and starting to slide away.

But his hand halted her. 'I know, or you would have ducked around the corner at the mere sight of me,' he drawled, still smiling.

She averted her face slightly, her eyes unable to meet his. 'Was it that obvious?'

He didn't bother to answer, but instead tilted her chin up, forcing her to look into his eyes, now filled with lazy charm and tender amusement. Her heart beat tumultuously, and she prayed that he couldn't hear it.

'Don't look so frightened,' he said, with the merest hint of playful mockery. 'I merely wanted to ask you if Ted apologised the way he was supposed to. I'm not going to tease you about your delightfully ardent reaction to my kiss.'

'Yes, he did, and why are you?' she retorted.

'Why am I what?'

'Teasing me.'

'I guess I am at that,' he said mildly. 'Perhaps because the memory lingered so very . . . very sweetly,' he added, tracing the line of her chin as he had the night before.

But this time she stepped back as if she were scalded. 'It won't happen again, I assure you. You're a very experienced lover, it's obvious, and a master at raising a woman's temperature, if she forgets herself . . . which I did for a moment.' She looked fully at him while somehow keeping her gaze and her voice steady. 'But I'm not a plaything and I refuse to be toyed with.'

'And now your emotions are in complete control, and you are fully armoured against my charms.' His voice was taunting. 'Right?'

'Right,' she said, and then carried on quickly, 'and I'd better go see what Suzy's up to.'

To her relief, this time he let her go, but only after giving her a slow, unnerving smile, cool and infuriatingly self-possessed. Silently cursing both him and fate, she retreated without even trying to return it.

As the evening wore on, she was able to push her worries to the back of her mind. One of the guests, a soft-spoken, unaffected woman named Elizabeth Shirley, had been a well-known singer years before, and as night came on, the other guests prevailed on her to sing some of the old Western ballads.

Elizabeth would sing the stanzas, her voice pure and silvery in the night air, and the rest would join in for the refrains, swaying slowly with the mournful, lovely melodies.

The final song was one Dawn had never heard before. In it a cowboy lamented the fencing in of the Texas range, the strange city people who flocked to the once-open land, and the other changes that signalled the passing of his era. This refrain Elizabeth sang alone:

> *It's gone for good, the unploughed range,*
> *For times must pass, and things must change.*
> *And I'm goin' too, but don't weep for me.*
> *I'm goin' where the wind blows free.*

The melody was haunting and Elizabeth's voice was achingly sweet, sending long, slow shivers down Dawn's back. The song had been written half a century before, and yet she could still look up and see a glorious profusion of gem-like stars through the clean night air. And around her, she knew, rolled an immense, virtually boundless, unploughed range; a range on which were real cowboys and wild mustangs, a vast land where the wind blew as free as ever it had.

As Elizabeth continued to sing to the hushed guests a sense of melancholy slowly grew in Dawn. Perhaps it was because Sam had told her that even a huge ranch like this seldom had a profitable year. Dan Kane could indulge himself in it because of his oil royalties. But how long would there be men like him to maintain ranches for the sheer joy of it as a way of life? When they stopped it would indeed be gone for good.

Or perhaps her gloom wasn't quite as high-minded as that. She was far too conscious of Dan Kane sitting close to Meg, one arm casually resting on the back of her chair. That in itself was enough to depress her. Finally, no longer able to maintain even a surface equilibrium, she excused herself from her companions despite a flattering chorus of male protests, and went to bed.

In the morning, the guests quickly dispersed. Dawn had been somewhat cheered when two of the young men she had danced with insisted she call them when she was next in San Antonio, and Duke Austin made her promise she and Suzy would visit him to see his art collection, but the melancholy of the night before lingered on.

Suzy, too, was down in the mouth without her new friends. Now that she knew the pleasures to be enjoyed with companions her own age, Dawn was sure Suzy was going to be less satisfied with only her company. It was natural for her to feel that way, and Dawn saw it as a healthy sign. But she wished Suzy had picked another afternoon to retreat to her room to read, leaving Dawn alone to dwell on the distressing developments of the last few days.

'Are you going up to the summer range this year, Daddy? Like you always do?' Suzy asked her father at dinner that night, with all the elaborate unconcern of a thirteen-year-old with an ulterior motive.

Dan Kane's eyebrows rose as he looked at his daughter. 'I suppose what you really want to know is if you and Dawn can come with me?' he asked.

'Could we? Please?' begged Suzy, and then rushed into an obviously well-rehearsed speech before her father could say a word. 'Last year you told me I was too young, and I needed to be older, and maybe I could go this year, and now it's this year.' Her eyes shone as she stopped for breath. 'Daddy, please?'

'Suzy, it's rough camping up there. There aren't beds, and there's no running water. But there *are* plenty of snakes,' he added, as his eyes flickered derisively over Dawn's face.

Dawn continued to eat, trying to pretend it didn't matter one way or the other to her. From what Sam had told her it sounded as if the cowboys up there lived exactly as they had a hundred years before. It would be the experience of a lifetime to go, and yet she was ambivalent about it. There was little privacy on a camping trip, so she wouldn't have to worry about finding herself alone with Dan Kane, but there would be an enforced intimacy with him—an intimacy she could do without.

Suzy was not to be diverted. 'Dawn wouldn't care. And I'll shake out her sleeping bag every night so there won't be any old snakes in it.'

Dan eyed his daughter sternly, then included Dawn in his frown. 'I'm warning you two right now: we'll be up there for two weeks, maybe three, and if either of you finds it too rough don't expect me to cart you home early,' he growled at his ecstatic offspring, who was blissfully unfazed by his threat.

His growl was unconvincing to Dawn's ears too. Her stomach knotted with apprehension. He hadn't put up much of a fight. Obviously, he must have planned on taking them all along. Why? He certainly couldn't be looking forward to having two females tagging along, unless . . . unless he was up to some sort of mischief. Disconcertingly, her mind went back to that unnerving smile in the atrium.

On second thoughts, she decided—not altogether convincingly—she was being silly. Sam had simply told him how much Suzy wanted to go; that was all. And a camping trip would be an ideal way to get through a few weeks of what seemed like an eternity stretching in front of her until September. The more she thought about it, in fact, the more she caught Suzy's excitement over it. The thing to do was simply to enjoy the experience and just do her level best to give a wide berth to snakes and other dangerous creatures.

Including Dan Kane.

# CHAPTER FIVE

It was as if Dan were making sure the trip was going to be rough, Dawn thought, clinging to the roll bar of the jeep as it bucketed and bounced through the cold, grey dawn. From the side-facing jump seat in the back, Dawn could see little but the dim shapes of mesquite and sage whipping by, and in the distance the dark, sharp silhouettes of the hills against the lightening sky. It was impossible to see the bumps and holes ahead, so she simply hung on for dear life. Dan could see them, though, and she was sure he wasn't even trying to avoid the worst of the potholes in the road—if you could call those bumpy ruts a road. Was he expecting, perhaps hoping, that she or Suzy would complain, so that he'd have an excuse to turn back to the ranch house and dump them out? Dawn glanced towards the front seats where Suzy, looking as if she were in seventh heaven, was sitting next to her father. Dan Kane was obviously going to have a long wait before his daughter complained about anything.

Dawn's jacket gave little protection against the cold wind buffeting the open jeep as it sped in the direction taken by the cattle drive. Brushing her wind-whipped hair out of her eyes for the hundredth time she debated on whether or not she should put it back in a sensible ponytail, but she decided not to. In just a few days, she had grown to love the feel of her hair freed, and wondered how she could have tied it back for so long. She closed her eyes and turned her face up to the clean wind.

The vague depression of the last few days was gone, and her newly-discovered zest for life had returned.

In the east the grey sky took on a clean blue tinge. They had been on the road for more than an hour and had left the house without even a cup of coffee, so her glances tended to linger on the food sack and thermos bottles. It would have been impossible to try to pour a cup of coffee, though, with the road so rough and Dan driving as if he were racing to a fire. And she wasn't going to be the first to suggest a breakfast stop, not with her growing feeling that Dan Kane was putting his daughter and her to an endurance test—one that he arrogantly expected them to fail.

Needing something to take her mind off the coffee, she studied the man who occupied so many of her thoughts lately. He was wearing a sleeveless down vest over his long-sleeved shirt, rather than a jacket, and he was hatless because of the wind. His wild, wind-tousled hair and the one-day shadow of a beard combined with his intense attention to the road to give him a grim, ferocious look. He's grouchy because he's hungry too, she thought, smiling. He's probably dying for a cup of coffee and doesn't want to admit it.

She hadn't realised she had laughed aloud until she saw him shoot a look at her through the rear-view mirror. Their gazes locked and he looked so bear-like that she couldn't help grinning.

'What's so funny?' he growled, glancing back at her over his shoulder. Suzy swivelled around too.

'Nothing's funny,' Dawn said evasively, then added, 'It's exciting to be at the start of an adventure. Weeks of living under the stars! It sounds fabulous.'

'Doesn't it?' agreed Suzy. 'I can't wait until we catch up with Sam.'

Dan downshifted the jeep and brought it to a halt. 'Hope you can wait long enough to stop for breakfast,' he said with a touch of asperity, as if he hadn't expected to be the first to suggest it.

'Sure, Daddy,' said Suzy, hopping out. 'I'll find us a picnic spot.'

Dawn picked up one of the thermos bottles and the large brown paper container that held breakfast. When she turned to jump out of the back, she was startled to find Dan standing there ready to help her down.

Wordlessly she took his offered hand and jumped down. Her legs, a little unsteady after the jogging ride, gave slightly under her, and she nearly lost her footing. Acutely conscious of the warmth and strength of his hands as he steadied her, she blushed, and was immediately flustered by the amusement that leaped to his eyes at her heightened colour.

'Thank you,' she said shortly, heartily wishing her temperature wouldn't rise so at the mere touch of his hands.

His eyes flickered over her, taking in her wind-tossed curls, her golden-brown eyes and the glow of soft peach in her cheeks. 'Very fetching, even in the morning,' he drawled, giving her a wicked, sardonic smile. He shook his head slowly back and forth in mock wonder. 'You sure bloomed with a vengeance.'

'Don't bother getting any ideas,' she retorted. 'Remember this is one blossom that's not available for the picking.'

'What? And leave all that beauty to wither on the vine?' he lamented, grinning.

Dawn glared briefly at him, then turned away as Suzy waved to them from atop a nearby rise.

'Up here!' she called.

Deliberately ignoring both Dan at her heels, and the thudding of her heart, Dawn scrambled up the slope. 'What a great spot!' she exclaimed, smiling at Suzy.

'Sure is, squirt,' Dan agreed, setting down the thermos and food sack. Dawn stiffened as he perched on a rock near her, flashing her a warm, lazy smile that set her every nerve tingling. But she was proud of the level look she forced herself to give him and of her polite but—she hoped—indifferent smile. Perhaps she should become an actress, Dawn thought somewhat ironically. By the end of the summer she would be quite good at it, if she were going to get this kind of practice.

Suzy dug into the sack at once. 'Oh boy, bacon, lettuce, and tomato sandwiches! My favourite!'

'What's the summer camp like?' Dawn asked Dan, as she poured the coffee while Suzy handed around sandwiches.

'It's not much,' he answered, shrugging. 'A corral for relief horses, a couple of campfire rings; a lean-to for the kitchen and mess table. That's about it.'

'It does sound pretty spartan,' Dawn agreed, unwrapping the waxed paper around her sandwich.

The flat rocks, warmed by the rays of the early morning sun, were a tranquil, perfect place to breakfast, and Dawn regained a measure of internal calm as she ate her fill of the thick heavenly-tasting sandwiches. The hot coffee chased off the last of her early morning chill, and she was able to give some of her attention to the beauty around them. The sun, growing brighter by the second, glinted on low, rugged hills mantled with mesquite and range grasses. Above them two hawks lazily wheeled in soaring circles, and all around them the sparkling air was alive with the chirping of sage sparrows flitting from bush to bush.

Shortly after their breakfast stop the road disappeared entirely, and Dan had to drive cross-country, so that it took them well over an hour to cover the last twenty miles of their fifty-mile journey. They drove past two or three loosely ranging groups of cattle before Dan pulled the jeep into the camp.

Dan had described it aptly; it wasn't much. When he parked the jeep near the rough corral, Dawn was delighted to see Paint among the relief horses.

Sam was waiting for them by the corral gate. 'What made you decide to bring these fillies along?' he asked Dan, winking soberly at Suzy.

'Tried to discourage them by telling them how rough it was up here, but you know women. Won't listen to a darn thing you tell them.'

Giggling, Suzy hugged Sam tightly, to his obvious pleasure and embarrassment.

Dan introduced Dawn to Hank, a rangy cowboy with a beer belly, who served as cook, and the three men started unloading the jeep.

'Paint's yours while you're here,' Sam called out to Dawn while they worked. 'Why don't you go say hello to him?'

Suzy and Dawn strolled over to the corral. To Dawn's delight, Paint came to her at once and gently nuzzled her jacket, looking for a treat. Laughing, she found the carrot she had brought for him. 'Between Sam and me, you're a very spoiled horse,' she said, stroking his powerful neck while his big, square teeth crunched the carrot.

'That's the truth,' Suzy agreed, and added with a sigh, 'I wish I could have brought Tandy along.'

'Talk about spoiled horses,' Dawn said, laughing. 'You'd put Persian rugs in Tandy's stall if your dad would let you.'

As soon as the jeep was unloaded, Hank whipped them up a hearty lunch of beans and freshly baked sourdough biscuits. When the meal was finished, Dan stood up. 'Let's go prowling, girls,' he said, strapping on a Smith & Wesson .38. Sam did the same, and both men slung Remington rifles in leather holders attached to their saddles.

Dan noted Dawn's surprised expression and raised an eyebrow. 'You wanted some adventure, didn't you? You never know when we might disturb a rattlesnake or run across a mountain lion that fancies us for dinner. It'll add a bit of excitement,' he said mockingly.

'You seem to forget,' she responded tartly, 'I'm country-bred and I'm well aware of the fact that unprovoked attacks by wild animals are rare.'

He merely grinned and mounted, then waited for Suzy and Sam to get on their horses. 'Everybody set? Let's go.'

'What's "prowling," Daddy?' Suzy asked as they started out.

'It's an old-fashioned word, squirt. Means riding the range and looking for any problems.'

'What kind of problems?'

'Overgrazing, water availability, things like that. And then the cattle have to be checked. There are a million diseases they can pick up out here.'

He patiently continued to answer all Suzy's questions, as well as the few Dawn couldn't resist asking. Frequently, he would stop just so they could observe the cowboys working. And once that afternoon they were lucky enough to come upon a couple of cowboys roping a steer to treat it on the spot for pink-eye. After one cowboy had roped it by the neck, another moved in to lasso a heel. The ends of the ropes were looped around the saddlehorns, and the cow was flopped onto its side and stretched out. The cowboys finished securing their ropes to their saddlehorns and leaped down, leaving it to the well-trained horses to keep the ropes taut while the men injected the steer with medicine and glued a patch of cloth over the eye.

When released, the animal stood bewildered for a moment, confused by the patch. Sympathetically, Dawn watched it shake its head in an unsuccessful attempt to dislodge the strange object. Finally, she was glad to see, it seemed to resign itself, and headed calmly back to the herd.

'Will they come back later to take it off?' she asked Dan, as they started to move on.

'It's not necessary,' he answered, riding next to her. 'It will fall off on its own in a week or two.'

Sometimes all four of them rode abreast; at other times they paired off in different combinations depending on the terrain. Dawn compelled herself to take no evasive action whenever she saw she was about to be paired with Dan, and by the end of the afternoon her strategy had begun to pay off. She found herself less apprehensive in his presence, and managed to maintain a façade so convincingly unruffled that she almost fooled herself.

The façade stayed intact. Perhaps, Dawn reflected in a moment of candour with herself, it was because Dan Kane made no effort to pierce it. But whether that was the reason or not, she didn't care. She was too busy enjoying herself as the days passed in a whirl. She couldn't decide what she enjoyed the most: the tantalising aroma of Hank's coffee and bacon awakening her, the sight of the magnificent canopy of stars glittering in the black velvet sky over her sleeping bag, or the feeling of excitement and contentment as the pages of her sketchbook leaped alive with cowboys roping, riding herd, or gossiping wearily around the campfire, tin mugs in hand. Perhaps it was all of it, combined with the growing closeness of her relationships with Suzy and Sam.

Oddly enough, it was only when Dan Kane was sleeping that his presence played havoc with her emotions. It was agony to lie in her sleeping bag night after night, knowing that his long form was stretched out just on the other side of the fire. Sometimes she'd awaken in the cool, silent blackness of the night to see the moon silvering his dark hair and casting strong shadows across the planes of his face. As unbidden memories of his kiss tortured her, she had to suppress the disgraceful and tormenting desire to reach out her hand and caress the clean, smooth line of his powerful jaw.

Tormented by the usual agonising dreams, she awakened well before dawn on the last day of the campout. As a result, she was the first to become aware of the threatening clouds sweeping across the sky and blotting out the stars.

Dan woke the instant she started to get out of her sleeping bag.

'No snakes, I hope?' he whispered.

'Funny, funny,' Dawn retorted lightly. 'I was only going to warn you that it looks like it's going to storm any minute.'

As if on cue a rumble of thunder punctuated her

sentence, awakening the others. Within seconds a jagged bolt of lightning split the sky, followed by a colossal clap of thunder so loud and sharp it made Dawn catch her breath. A few fat raindrops splattered on the ground around them, turning into a torrential downpour by the time they had hurriedly gathered up their bags and gear and scurried into the lean-to.

Except for the knowledge that these wild, night-time storms could create chaos among the stock, scattering the terrified animals in all directions, Dawn would have revelled in the display provided by a southwestern thunderstorm in all its glory. And this one was stupendous. Her fingers itched to put its beauty on paper, but it would have been impossible. There was no way she could capture the ear-splitting rolls of thunder that seemed to shake the very ground, or the crackling hiss of the brilliant flashes of lightning that lit up the whole sky.

The storm passed almost as quickly as it had come. By sunrise it was over and Dan and his foreman, with Dawn and Suzy in tow, spent the morning assessing the damage. It was almost lunchtime when they reached the furthest herd. Near the peacefully grazing cows they saw a tall, lanky cowboy squatting on his heels in front of a dead steer.

'Broken leg, Mike?' asked Dan when they rode up to the cowboy. 'Did you have to shoot it?'

'Nope,' replied the cowhand, 'already dead. Lightning. I was just trying to decide what to do with him.'

'I don't think he's good for anything but tonight's dinner,' responded Dan philosophically. 'Many problems with the herd?'

'Problems!' snorted the cowboy, rising. 'When the lightning hit this poor critter, he was right dang in the middle of the herd. The whole lot of them scattered before Ferdie or me could do a damn thing. Oh, it was fierce.'

'These things happen,' commiserated Sam. 'I know you did the best you could.'

'Well, we managed to round up most of them,' explained Mike, 'but we're about a hundred head short. Ferdie took off east to see if he could pick up a few more. Soon as our relief men show up, I'll send them out too. I think we're all going to have to rough it tonight.'

Since word had got around that Hank was preparing a feast for the boss's and the girls' last night, the offer to stay out was doubly generous. Usually half of the hands spent the night in camp fortifying themselves with Hank's delicious and hearty meals while the rest camped out near the herds, dependent on their own meagre cooking skills.

'I appreciate it, Mike,' Dan said, 'and I'll make it up to all of you. Tell you what, though. Sam and I can do some looking around with the girls. We'll report back here if we spot any of them. That'll cut down your search.'

'Thanks, boss,' Mike said.

'Sam, you take the squirt here and check out that box canyon behind Humpback Ridge.' Casually, without looking at Dawn, he added, 'Dawn and I'll head down along Verde River for a few miles, near where we found those two calves a couple of years ago. No sense in the four of us trying to team up again. We'll see you back at camp.'

Without further words, and with only the briefest glance in Dawn's direction to make sure she was following Dan headed off. As if she had any choice in the matter, she thought wryly. For a couple of hours they rode into a biting wind that made conversation almost impossible, and although they saw no cattle, there were many hoof prints, and Dan followed them further and further from camp. Dawn was chilled and hungry, and the wind had stiffened her fingers on the reins. She was thinking of asking him to stop, at least long enough to get out of the saddle and have something to eat, when they came to a low rise.

'The Verde River,' Dan said, as they looked down on the broad, sandy, and rock-strewn river bed. Forged during the flood years, it was a good hundred feet wide, while the serpentine river itself, though turbulent and swollen from the storm, could only have been about twenty feet across. 'Shall we stop for lunch on the other side?'

'Yes, please. I'm hungry and cold,' Dawn confessed.

'We'll soon fix that,' he said, giving her a lazy smile. Then, surprisingly, he added, 'Did I ever tell you that, although you might be the most stubborn female I've ever met, you're also the most uncomplaining?'

Dawn smiled in return and shook her head, while inside she felt an unaccustomed warm glow. 'No, you didn't. But I'll remind you to tell me—next time I incur your disfavour,' she teased.

Dan laughed. 'I'll ford first,' he said, 'just in case there are any problems. Then you follow.'

Dawn watched Dan's animal gingerly enter the river. It was faster and deeper than it looked and she was surprised to see the water lap at his stirrups. Nevertheless, he crossed with no difficulty, and reining in his horse under a gnarled and spreading oak tree on the other side, he turned.

'Just give Paint his head and hold on,' he called, 'and you'll be all right.'

Dawn urged Paint forward, but when they reached the water, she pulled up the reins, and looked uncertainly at the river. Inexplicably, her skin crawled in a shiver of apprehension. Stroking the animal's warm neck, she could feel the twitching muscles that told her he too was nervous. How silly we're both being, she thought to herself; it really wasn't dangerous, and they'd be over in a few seconds. And she certainly wasn't about to complain to Dan Kane about his fording spot, after his compliment of a moment ago.

She patted the horse once more. 'Okay, boy,' she murmured, digging her heels into his sides to urge him forward. Paint warily entered the water. About halfway across the horse shuddered violently and veered to his right.

'Pull him back!' Dan shouted in dead earnest. 'There's a drop-off downstream!'

Dawn was tugging hard on the left rein when she heard a soft splash near the half-exposed oak roots a few feet away. And then there it was, in the water: a blotched, muddy-brown body undulating swiftly towards her; a horrible, open, grey-white mouth. Whinnying frenziedly and showing the whites of his eyes, Paint reared away from the writhing water-moccasin, wildly pummelling the air with his hooves.

Normally it would have taken more than a rearing horse to unseat her, but the sight of the deadliest of Southwestern snakes paralysed her. Unbelievably, her wooden fingers refused to grasp the reins, her knees could not be made to grip Paint's heaving sides, her very mind would not obey. Fainting, she felt herself sliding from the saddle, falling as if in slow motion towards the hideous, squirming thing below.

She heard herself scream, and then her nose and mouth were filled with churning water. A confused ferment of images and sounds—pistol shots, flailing horse's hooves, her own screams and thrashings—engulfed her, and then two strong arms were scooping her up.

'It's all right now, baby. It's gone. Everything's all right.'

Weeping with relief, she let her head fall to Dan's shoulder and wrapped her arms tightly around his neck as he carried her from the river. On the bank he stood holding her in his arms for what seemed a long time while she buried her forehead in the hollow of his neck, grateful for the warmth of his broad chest.

When she finally looked up he gently lowered her legs to the ground. 'Okay, now?' he asked hoarsely, holding her close. 'You've had quite a scare.'

'Is it dead? Did you shoot it?' she asked, shuddering.

'No, I was a bit more interested in not hitting *you* than in hitting it. But between your screams, Paint's hooves, and my shots, it took off, thinking, no doubt, that retreat was the better part of vâlour.' Drily he added, 'Unfortunately our horses thought so too.'

Dawn was suddenly aware that her arms were still around his neck and quickly let them drop. 'Thanks for rescuing me. I'm fine now,' she said shakily, breaking away from his grip, but on the first step her legs quivered and threatened to give way, and he shot his arm around her again. He led her to a large flat rock and made her sit down. 'Put your head between your knees.'

She did so and felt her strength return as the blood moved to her head. She looked up abruptly. 'What did you mean about our horses?'

'I mean they're gone,' he said. 'Hightailed it downriver. They're probably still running.'

'But that's awful! How will we—?'

He shrugged his unconcern. 'Do you know how few

water-moccasins there are around here?' he said with exasperation. 'Of course, I should have known if there was even one, it'd find you.'

'Are you sure it's gone?' She clenched her jaws to keep her teeth from chattering. Belatedly, she realised she was not only frightened but very cold. The wind had increased in sharpness, and she was wet through.

'Yes, I'm sure, but if it will make you feel any better we'll build our fire further downstream.'

'Why are we going to build a fire?' she asked nervously, as the potential ramifications of their situation began to occur to her. 'Shouldn't we start walking back?'

'No,' he said firmly. 'You need warmth. You're soaked, and you're shaking like a leaf.'

'But how—?'

'Fortunately, you were riding Paint. Knowing him, he'll find his way back to camp and the boys will track him back to us. Let's just hope he goes straight back. There are only four or five hours of daylight left.'

Dawn's face clouded. 'And if he doesn't, what will we do?' she asked, her heart in her mouth.

He laughed. 'Find some shelter for the night and settle in.'

'This isn't a laughing matter,' she snapped, jittery and on edge. She wasn't sure whether it was the thought of that awful snake somewhere nearby or the possibility of spending the night alone with Dan that frightened her more.

Dan grinned. 'I thought you were immune to my charms,' he said mockingly, reading her thoughts. 'If not, you've certainly been giving a good imitation of it these last couple of weeks. At any rate, we'll probably get rescued, so don't panic yet,' he added, his blue eyes gleaming with sardonic humour.

At the sight of the colour flooding her cheeks, he laughed shortly and started unbuttoning his shirt.

'What are you doing?' Dawn asked, astounded, her heart accelerating with alarm.

'Taking off my shirt. What does it look like?'

'I know that.' She looked angrily into his dancing blue eyes. 'Damn you, I know that!' She bit her lip; it wasn't like her to talk like that to anyone, under any circumstances. The façade she had so carefully erected had crumbled and she was at the edge of her self-control.

He pulled the heavy denim shirt off and tossed it to her. 'Put it on. I have no intention of having you die of exposure, even if you are an ungrateful little wretch. I'm going to get some wood.'

Almost in tears again, Dawn waited until he was a good distance away before she stripped off her soaked clothing with numbed fingers and slipped into his shirt. Fortunately, it was huge and hung below her hips, and was damp only where he had held her against him. Even the little warmth it gave her made her feel better and brought back her good sense. She was really overreacting to the situation. Paint loved the evening lump of sugar that was always given to him by Sam, so he was probably eagerly making for camp right now. And with the ground so wet, his hooves would leave a trail a child could follow.

Reassured but still shivering, she pulled at her wet and waterlogged boots. It was a struggle to wrench them off, but the relief was immediate. The sand was warmer than the air, and she wiggled her toes luxuriously in it.

'Come on over here!' she heard him call.

Oh dear, she thought in alarm, looking at the rock-strewn ground; taking off those boots had been a mistake. 'It's going to take me a while to get my boots back on!' she shouted back. 'Where are you?'

The muffled sound of masculine cursing briefly hung in the air. Then his lean, bare-chested figure appeared at the crest of a low, sandy hill.

He strode to her, gathered up her clothing and boots, and thrust them into her hands. Then he stood scowling at her for a moment, bent down, and brusquely picked her up.

'Put me down!' she gasped, clutching her things.

'Be quiet. I'm beginning to think you're more trouble than you're worth.'

There was nothing she could do. Besides, she had to admit that the heat of his body against her was delicious. He carried her quickly and with ease, and she was almost disappointed when they arrived at a small cove in the river bank, in front of which he had piled up some wood. He dropped her with about as much ceremony as he'd dump a sack of potatoes and turned to light the tinder at the base of the pile.

Dawn wished she hadn't thought of potatoes; it had been a long time since she'd eaten. It was too bad the saddle bag with her lunch hadn't fallen off Paint when she did.

'We're in luck,' Dan said after the flame had caught. 'These concave walls will reflect back the heat from the fire and we should be toasty enough. No mountain lions can sneak up on us either, if we do wind up spending the night,' he added in a amused drawl.

'If you're saying that to scare me, don't bother. I'm already scared enough,' Dawn declared, drawing strength somehow from her very fear. 'If you think I'm going to spend the night here with you, you're crazy. You're going to have to figure out something else.'

He rose from his crouch at the fire, resting his hands on his hips and looming over her with more than a touch of menace. Surveying her insolently, he said, 'Considering that it was *you* that fell off your horse like some silly greenhorn and got us into this mess, and considering it's *you* that's snuggled up in my nice warm shirt while I'm freezing, I'd say you're taking a lot for granted.'

Dawn was instantly contrite. What he'd said was absolutely true. All she'd had to do was sit on her horse and Paint would have carried her to safety. 'I'm sorry,' she whispered, chastened. Her eyes dropped. 'I guess I've been . . .' Her voice trailed off as she heard him slowly approach her. He tilted up her chin, forcing her to look up at him.

'You think you're frightened at the thought of spending the night alone with me?' he said, his voice hard. 'Well, I'm the one who should be worried. That damn water-moccasin would be less dangerous than you.'

Astonishingly, his mouth captured hers in a hard, punishing kiss, his arms enclosing her to prevent her flight. With her heart pounding wildly, she tried at first to push him away, but then, as his kiss softened from one of anger to one of gentleness, her arms of their own volition found their way around his neck. As on the night of the party, Dawn lost track of everything except sensations: the feel of his lips draining her resistance, the hardness of his body, the weakness in her knees, the pounding beat of hot blood pulsing at her temples.

'Dan . . .' she managed, 'please . . .'

Softly, his arms loosened. For a long, breathless moment he looked at her with something she'd never seen in his face before. Affection? Tenderness, even? Before it had really registered, the familiar hard expression, returned to those flinty eyes. He turned abruptly and walked from the cove. 'I'd better see about hunting us up a rabbit,' he called carelessly over his shoulder.

# CHAPTER SIX

A BEWILDERING whirl of emotions enveloped Dawn as she watched his retreating back. She was head over heels in love with him, and had been since the night of the party. But she'd been fighting the knowledge, she thought desolately, because loving Dan Kane wasn't going to bring her anything but heartache. She wasn't from his world, and her chances of being asked to marry him were about as good as old Paint's.

Dawn burst into tears. For many minutes she pillowed her head on her arms and let them flow unchecked. Then, little by little, she got control of herself; being hopelessly in love was bad enough without having to suffer the agony of having that love revealed. Which was exactly what would happen if Dan returned and found her like this. She was going to get hold of herself before he returned, Dawn vowed resolutely to herself as she fought down the tears, even if it killed her. Leaden-hearted, and with no more than a tenuous control of her surface emotions, she went down to the river's edge and splashed cool water on her face to wash away the traces of the tears.

Calmer, her breathing no longer ragged, she returned to the cove and added more wood to the fire. Then she glanced around almost frantically for something, anything, to do to ward off the thoughts that were so ready to return and would so easily give her away. Her eyes rested on a forked branch in the woodpile in front of her. If she could locate another of about the same size she could rig up a spit and drape her clothes on it in front of the fire. Although it might take forever to get the jeans dry, the shirt wouldn't take long at all. Then at least she could give Dan's back. If she was cold, he must be frozen.

She quickly located the other forked branch she needed, dug two holes near the fire and stuck the branches upright into the ground. A circle of stones around each stick stabilised it, and a straight branch rested perfectly in the forks. She draped her shirt and socks over it and spread her jeans on the ground, arranging her boots beside them.

Her handiwork looked enough like a cooking spit to remind her how hungry she was, and she didn't push away the images of roasting hens and rabbits. She might as well torture herself with a desire that *did* have a chance of being fulfilled, Dawn reflected with bleak humour, and let her mind conjure up the sounds and smells of slowly turning, sizzling, smoking meat. The strategy worked too well; in a very short time she was downright famished.

When she heard a muffled shot in the far distance she was pleased, hoping Dan had hit the world's largest rabbit. Her eyes fell on a wild sage plant growing on the bank. Delighted, she gathered several leafy stalks and brought them back. They'd go well with rabbit. Then, noting the time, she sat down in front of the fire, feeling a bit like Mrs Neanderthaler waiting for her mate to return home with a mastodon for dinner.

Half an hour went by and there was no sign of him. She began to feel jittery. What could be taking him so long? The high, yipping sound of a coyote broke the silence and was followed by a mournful, spine-chilling howl. A second coyote joined in and then a third. It was a pack. Dawn's worry grew, although she knew they'd steer clear of the fire. She resisted the impulse to toss on more wood; it might have to last them the night.

Where was Dan? Minutes dragged like hours, and she found herself looking at her watch almost constantly. At every rattle of bush or scrabble in the sand she looked up fearfully, expecting a mountain lion or a snake to be glaring at her, but finding only a horned toad and a tiny green lizard. Another half-hour crawled by. Needles of worry jabbed at her, and grew, and became a wrenching fear that constricted her heart. What if the shot she'd heard had been accidental? What if the gun had gone off, wounding him, when he'd stumbled over a rock? He could be lying out there bleeding to death. Or he could have been bitten by that water-moccasin and already be . . . be dead?

Unable to sit still any longer, she jumped up and ran a little down-river despite the wind and the sharp pebbles, and anxiously raked the distance for him. There was nothing; only windswept range and angry grey sky.

Two hours ago she would have done anything to avoid being alone with him, and now she'd give anything she had just to know he was safe.

Dawn heard the sound of him scrambling down the river bank before she saw him. Mindless of anything but the fact that he was alive, she flew to him, laughing and crying at the same, and threw herself into his arms, burying her face in his shoulder.

'Hey, what's all this?' he asked in genuine astonishment.

'I . . . I thought something might have happened to you,' Dawn said weakly, pulling back in sudden mortification. 'I heard your shot ages and ages ago.' Then she added lamely, 'I imagined all sorts of terrible things.'

He casually draped an arm around her shoulder and they turned and walked back towards the fire. 'It's probably just your empty stomach,' he said teasingly. Obviously, her impulsive hug had disarmed him; there was a gentle warmth in his voice. 'Everything always seems twice as scary when you're hungry.' He held up the partridge she hadn't noticed he was carrying in his other hand.

'Food!' she cried joyfully. Suddenly she felt marvellous. Dan was safe beside her, the fire was cosy and inviting, and tomorrow could take care of itself.

'I only winged it,' he confessed with a grin. 'It took me practically an hour to hunt it down finally. It's a rather small—'

'It's perfect!' Dawn took the bird from him and a pocket knife as well. 'Go warm up by the fire while I get it ready.'

Plucking chickens and game birds had been her least-liked job at home, but all that practice had at least made her fast. It didn't take her long to clean the bird and prepare it for cooking.

Dan had taken his boots off and was comfortably stretched out in front of the fire, propped up on one arm. Golden-skinned, with his graceful but powerful neck and his lithe, well-muscled torso, he was a magnificent sight, and her throat caught just to look at him. The man was too darn good-looking and magnetic for his own good. Or hers. She really should have known better than to accept his job offer in the first place, she scolded herself.

'Are you going to stand there all afternoon?' he asked mockingly.

'Only thinking about cooking logistics,' she said lightly, glad he was too far away to see her blush. She tested the shirt and socks on the spit, and was pleased to see that they were dry. The jeans, however, seemed as wet as ever.

'If you promise you won't look,' she said, 'I'll change shirts and give you back yours.'

'Not even one peek?' he asked playfully.

'You'd better watch out, Dan Kane, or I'll keep them both,' she taunted. Moving behind him and out of his line of sight, she quickly changed shirts, somewhat disconcerted to find that her own covered up much less of her. Why, she wondered, does one feel completely proper—well, almost—in a bikini bathing suit, and terribly improper, to say the least, wearing a shirt and a pair of bikini underpants in front of a man? They weren't nearly so revealing, after all.

Dropping his shirt on him as she passed by, she got intently to work over the cooking to cover her shyness. Deftly, she twined the sage around the bird, skewered it on the spit, and lit a small pile of wood directly underneath it. She felt him watching her and finally had to look up. His eyes were mischievous.

'One would swear you've done this before.'

'What . . . been stranded in the middle of nowhere with a man, or roasted a bird on a spit?'

'Roasted a bird on a handmade spit, of course,' he said. 'You look far too innocent for the former.'

This time he was close enough to see her flush, and he laughed.

'A woman can spend the night alone with a man and still remain innocent,' she said as coolly as she could manage under his freely roving gaze. 'As you'll soon find out if we don't get rescued.'

'I was afraid you'd say that,' he said with a wry grin. Then his eyes softened. 'Tell me about him.'

'Him?' she asked, bewildered.

'The man who sent you scurrying into the shell.'

Dawn frowned faintly and shrugged. 'It was a boy, not a man, and it was nothing much, really,' she answered evasively, staring back at the fire. That was certainly the truth, she thought forlornly. Now that she knew what it meant to be truly miserable, what had happened to her six years ago seemed hardly worth talking about. How extraordinary that she had permitted it to drive her into the shell that Dan talked about so often and so accurately.

'Little things become big things when you lock them up inside.'

She could feel his eyes fixed on her.

'How old were you?'

'Seventeen,' she answered reluctantly, 'and I assure you, you'd find my childish little tribulations boring.'

'Nothing about you could possibly bore me, so stop being mysterious and tell me.'

Flustered by his words, yet bridling at his command-ing tone, she looked uncertainly up at him and was surprised to discover that his blue eyes were gentle and accepting. On impulse she decided to tell him. Talking about the remote, dead past seemed a great deal safer than some other conversational topics that might come up.

'You were right that afternoon when you said no woman gets to the age of twenty-three without discover-ing she has the—how did you put it?—the ideal figure?' Dawn said, resting her eyes again on the flickering flames. 'I didn't even get to fifteen. And it didn't take very many dates to find out that young men have only one thing on their minds,' she said drily, reaching out and giving the spit a quarter turn. 'It's funny how my girlfriends envied me, and they could hardly believe I was serious when I stopped dating. But I did—I just didn't want to fend off any more clumsy embraces—until I was seventeen, and Ron Morris began to pay attention to me.'

'What made him so special?' Dan asked quietly.

'His manner, I guess. He was a complete gentleman and a top-notch student too, and a three-letter athlete. You know, one of those all-round types that can do anything they put their minds to. And he seemed genuinely interested in my companionship and brilliant conversation,' Dawn said with irony in her voice.

It was strange to talk about it with so little emotion; almost as if it had happened to someone else.

'He took me out for six weeks without demanding more than a chaste goodnight kiss. Needless to say, I fell in love with him.' She smiled wanly at herself. 'Pretty soon I was actually wishing for a little *more* passion on his part.' Her voice trailed off.

'Until?' Dan murmured gently. His eyes, so surprisingly attentive and soft, had never left her face.

'Until I accidentally overheard two girls gossiping about Ron.' Here she faltered for the first time. This part would never be easy to talk about. She fixed her eyes on the fire and ploughed ahead. 'They said he had a bet with a friend that . . .' Her voice trailed off again.

'That he'd be the first to give you a tumble in the hay, and all the gentlemanly attentions were merely his technique to get you there.'

Dawn looked at him in mute surprise.

'Don't look so amazed,' he said with a gentle smile. 'That's a pretty common sort of bet among boys that age. Anyway, was it true? I know you, you confronted him with it.'

'Yes. At first he tried to deny it, but then he confessed.' She paused and added ruefully, 'If I'd been as mature emotionally as I was physically, I would have learned a good lesson and taken it philosophically, I suppose. Instead, I went flying into my shell and never came out.' Until you came along, she added to herself.

As she finished talking, Dawn could hear her words hanging in the air. The whole episode rang trivial now in her ears, foolish and adolescent—especially before this man whose experience with love had been so much more devastating.

Suddenly angry at him and herself, she stared defiantly at him. 'Satisfied? Now you can laugh.'

Dan looked exasperated. 'It's never funny when a person's hurt,' he said. 'But not many people are hurt as fortunately as you. You ought to be grateful to that jerk.'

Her eyes widened. 'Grateful? What do you mean?'

'If it hadn't been for him you would have been like a million other girls. You would have been . . .' He frowned, looking into the fire. 'Well, you wouldn't have been you.'

Dawn didn't know what he meant, but she knew it was a compliment, and she didn't know how to handle compliments from Dan Kane. She dropped her eyes to stare into the fire. The sound of him moving towards her mingled with the crackling of the reddish-orange flames, which leaped and darted as the hot juices of the partridge trickled down on them. He gently pushed aside the veil of honey-coloured hair, alive with reflected highlights from the fire, that hid her face from him.

'You *are* every man's dream of a beautiful woman,' he said softly. 'But beautiful women face pitfalls, and not many avoid them. You have.'

His touch and his nearness made her heart lurch, and she was unable to hide her trepidation as she looked up at him. 'Pitfalls?' she repeated faintly.

'Yes, pitfalls. An early marriage before you'd had a chance to make a mature choice, or worse . . .' His visage darkened as he went on, '. . . You could have had your head turned by all the male attention, and become a narcissistic, superficial ninny with no thought for anyone but herself.'

'Like your first wife?' The words came out on their own before she could choke them back. Dawn tensed, expecting an angry reaction. She saw his jaw tighten, but he answered lightly enough.

'Exactly. I couldn't have dragged her up here to spend a couple of weeks camping; not in a million years. The sun would have ruined her complexion or she might have broken a fingernail and ruined her manicure.' His voice hardened. 'She was all tinsel, and I fell for her like a brick. Marrying her was like opening up the shiniest, prettiest box under the Christmas tree and finding a rat inside.' The lines of his mobile features turned grim. 'We hadn't been married long before I discovered she'd lied about all the important things; about wanting a family— Suzy was an accident—and about loving ranch life. Her idea of living was to lead a jet-set sort of existence at whatever gambling spot she happened to fancy.' Dan shrugged. 'But for me, the timing and the whole rotten deceit were lethal. I don't think I could trust another woman as long as I live.'

The words seemed to shrivel her soul, so much so that she physically winced.

Dan reached out and pulled her into his arms. 'Hey, don't look like that.' He slid his mouth over her hair until his lips delicately traced the curve of her ear. 'I forgot for a moment I was talking to a female. You should take it as a compliment that I see you as a person first, and a ravishing, maddeningly seductive woman second. Well, not always second,' he muttered thickly, as his mouth continued on a path to her lips. Soon he was kissing her throat, her cheeks, and then claiming her lips again.

Dawn felt herself dissolving under the sweetness of his caresses. Her body went limp and yielding as her blood sang in her ears, and her lips parted helplessly under the demands of his mouth. She was being forced slowly back onto the warm, soft sand, but was unable to protest. The exquisitely sweet sensations roused by his long, powerful body lying half over hers were almost painful in their intensity. Something stirred deep inside her, something long dormant. Her hands clung tightly to his shoulders as her body instinctively arched upward. Without thought, her lips responded hungrily to his.

Dawn heard Dan moan huskily as his hands unbuttoned her shirt. She closed her eyes and gave herself over to her unparalleled feelings as his hands caressed the taut, rosy tips of her breasts and then closed possessively over them. Desire swept through her like a brush fire. She buried her hands in his hair, hearing the rapid beating of his heart above her as his lips followed the burning trail of his hand, and his mouth kissed her naked breasts. The caress of his tongue sent wild new flames to nerve endings she didn't know she possessed. Fires . . . flames . . . smoke . . .

*Smoke?* My God, something was burning!

'The partridge!' they both gasped simultaneously, then broke into shaky laughter.

Dan, breathing roughly, looked down into her overheated face, but Dawn couldn't meet his gaze. And she couldn't stop trembling. She pushed herself away from him and sat up, quickly buttoning her blouse. Thankful for the diversion, she fled to extinguish the flames.

She had to be out of her mind! If she wasn't a great deal more careful in the future, she was going to drop like a ripe plum right into Dan Kane's hand, to be toyed with at whim. Still caught off balance and discomposed by how easily she had dissolved under his formidable technique, Dawn looked reluctantly back at him to see him leaning casually on one elbow. The wicked glint was back in his blue eyes.

She stared defiantly back at him. 'Don't be misled by . . . by what just happened.'

'Misled? In what way?' he asked innocently, as his eyes devoured her.

'It won't happen again,' she said firmly, hoping she sounded a great deal more confident than she felt.

'I know,' he drawled, his mouth curving in a faint smile. 'I can tell that I leave you completely cold by your lack of response.'

Dawn shot him a furious glance. 'I have no intention of having an affair with you,' she asserted heatedly. Her heart pounded erratically as she said it. Intention or not, she had just come perilously close.

Groping to change the subject, she turned back to the meat, and the game she'd played with herself before. 'It's only a little bit scorched,' she said. 'I wish we had something to go with it. I'd love some wild rice.'

'Is that what you'd love?' he said, grinning.

'And corn,' she went on, pretending to ignore him, 'dripping with fresh butter. And pecan pie for dessert.' He looked so confident and smug she wished she had the courage to throw something at him.

'Stop it, woman,' he cried, laughing, 'you'll drive me crazy. Just how many of my appetites do you intend to toy with?' He laughed again as a wash of colour rose on her cheeks. 'This bird had better be good after what it cost me,' he added ruefully. 'Or do I mean lost me?'

But Dawn refused to be drawn onto that dangerous ground again. 'It should be ready soon,' was all she murmured.

Finally the bird took on a golden hue—on the unburnt side—and she pronounced it ready. The oils from the sage had lightly seasoned the tough but flavourful meat, and soon nothing was left of the bird but a pile of bones.

'Absolutely delicious, burnt part and all,' Dan commented. 'I only wish we had about three more.'

'Me, too,' agreed Dawn, not quite truthfully. Actually, food was no longer on her mind. The sun was almost down and her thoughts were racing ahead to the dangerous prospects in store for her if someone didn't come soon.

They walked down to the water's edge to wash. The early evening air had grown increasingly cold, and Dawn was chilled by the time they returned to the fire. Dan tossed some more wood on it, while Dawn stood before it warming herself, trying to look casual and relaxed. But every nerve was strung tight as she listened for anything that might indicate an approaching rescuer. When she actually did hear a faraway, faint drumming, she thought a wishful imagination was playing tricks on her, but the sound soon enough became recognisable. Hoofbeats!

Dan heard them, too, and when she heard him swear under his breath, she couldn't resist laughing in sheer relief.

He smiled too, but with a sardonic gleam in his eyes. 'You think you're escaping from me, Dawn, but it's yourself you're escaping from. You'll stop running eventually—when you finally discover it's your own desire you're running from, not mine.' The smile disappeared. 'I want you,' he said, mocking and menacing both, 'and I intend to have you.'

Then he turned and waved casually to Sam and the cowhands as they came into sight across the river.

Dawn turned on the hot water full blast, then adjusted the cold water just enough so that she wouldn't be scalded. An ambrosial lavender fragrance rose in the steam as she poured bubble bath oil into the gushing water. With a sigh of pleasure she stepped in as soon as the tub was full and stretched out until only her head was not submerged.

This had to be the best thing about spending two weeks without plumbing, she reflected, soaking in the velvety water. The once-commonplace hot bath now seemed the height of extravagance and outright hedonism. Moulding a fluffy mound of iridescent bubbles, she sighed again at her jumbled thoughts.

The last night at the summer camp had been as festive as a party, once she and Dan had shown up unharmed. To her relief Suzy had taken their misadventure in her stride.

'I knew you were all right,' Suzy had said, spontaneously hugging Dawn, 'because you were with Daddy.'

'Oh yes,' Dawn managed. 'Perfectly safe. As safe as could be.' About as safe as a chinchilla in a fur coat factory!

Hank, ladle in hand, approached. 'Bet you two could stand a cup of coffee before dinner—'

'I'll get it,' Suzy offered, scampering away.

'For a while,' Hank muttered with a deadpan expression, 'I was afraid all my fancy cooking was going to waste.' His face broke into a grin. ''Til Sam pointed out if they didn't find you two tonight, we'd already have the vittles for a shotgun wedding.'

There was a brief silence, during which the shuffling of Sam's boots and the clearing of Sam's throat were all that could be heard.

Dawn bit back a smile at the dark look Dan flashed his foreman. 'I'd sure appreciate it,' he said, 'if you men did a hell of a lot less talking and a hell of a lot more work when I'm not around.'

The last few bubbles in her hands popped, bringing Dawn back to the present, and to her dilemma. Dan Kane was pursuing her and she knew it wouldn't lead to marriage. He'd made his feelings about that institution quite clear. So what was she to do? In her heart she knew: resign from his employment and get back to San Antonio, however she had to do it. Yet the thought of leaving the Rocking K and never seeing him again was more than she could bear. He had read her like a book, all right; she wanted him every bit as much as he wanted her.

She sat up with a splash. He'd been right about one thing he'd said by the fire that afternoon. She was a mature woman, and she knew what she wanted out of life. Dan Kane had to desire her—she wanted that—but he also had to love her, as much as she loved him. And more than that, he had to trust her as well, enough to exchange wedding vows with her. She would settle for nothing less. Dawn stepped firmly from the tub and vigorously towelled herself dry.

For the first time since the morning she'd sat drawing in the courtyard of the Alamo—that awful, wonderful morning when he'd strolled so nonchalantly into her life—she felt a real measure of calm. With a growing peace she slipped on a robe, then spread out her rough sketches on the carpet. They were good; better than she'd realised. If nothing else, her summer on the Rocking K would provide her with years of material to work from in the future.

She picked a quick sketch she had done of Suzy grooming Tandy. Finished, it would make a nice present to give the child when she left for boarding school. It was late, but Dawn didn't want to go to sleep yet. The grip she had on her waking mind was one thing, but her dreams were another matter entirely. She pulled out some fine, heavy drawing paper and her box of charcoals and went to work.

It was well after midnight when she finally went to bed, but barely daylight when she woke. Fully alert in seconds, she flung the sheet from her and got out of bed. It looked like a battlefield, she thought ruefully, looking at the tangled sheets, and in a way it had been. As she'd feared, she'd wrestled with appallingly sensual dreams of Dan all through the night.

She resolutely pushed them out of her mind and dressed. Quietly, she went to her work area in the living room, taking her half-finished drawing with her. When Dan strolled in just before breakfast the drawing lacked nothing but the finishing touches.

'Have trouble sleeping?' he asked, raising an eyebrow at the sight of her working so early. 'You should have looked me up. I would have given you a back rub,' he said teasingly, as he came to look over her shoulder at what she was working on.

'I don't think it would have put me to sleep,' she retorted drily, unable to keep herself from blushing. Darn him, she reflected angrily, seven o'clock in the morning was too early for blushing.

'Perhaps not.' An infuriating smile tugged at his lips. 'But it would have been a pleasant way to stay awake.'

'I spent my time quite pleasantly, thank you,' she replied coolly.

'And productively, too,' he said, suddenly serious. He studied her drawing for a few moments. 'You know, your lines become more assured every day, and you seem to need fewer of them to capture an image.'

'Thank you,' she said softly, disarmed by the unexpected compliment. 'It's going to be a present for Suzy, for her dorm room at school—if she likes it, that is.'

'She'll like the drawing, all right; it's getting her back east *to* a dorm room that's worrying me. I was hoping that if I took her up to the summer range and worked her as hard as my dad used to work me, she'd start to think school wasn't so bad. Instead, she absolutely thrived.' He spoke glumly, but there was obvious admiration in his voice. 'Oh, I knew she loved to ride and all, but I've never given her any responsibilities before. She acted as if I was doing her a favour giving her work—even the day I made her rake the manure out of the corral.'

Dawn smiled. 'If you ask me, you're just finding out she's a chip off the old block,' she said crisply. 'She loves the Rocking K as much as you do, and going east to school is about the same as being banished to Siberia.'

He moved his shoulders in an impatient shrug and frowned. 'I'm beginning to get that message. By the way, Duke Austin called last night. He's having some people over for dinner next Friday. We're invited.'

'We?' she said, puzzled.

'You, me and Suzy. He made a special point of asking you, and I took the liberty of accepting for you. I know you'll enjoy seeing his art collection. And you're going to want to meet one of his guests.'

'One of his guests?'

'Buck Harvey.'

'Buck Harvey?' she cried, thunderstruck. Her eyes were sparkling with excitement.

'I'm beginning to feel,' Dan said, 'as if I'm in an echo chamber.'

'Really?' Dawn said. 'Buck Harvey? The artist?'

'In the flesh.' Dan grinned. 'Now how about some breakfast?'

Four other aircraft were already parked at the end of the airstrip on Duke Austin's Double Bar D Ranch when Dan brought their plane down.

'That's the Haagsons' plane,' said Suzy, excitedly pointing to a small Learjet. Suzy had been looking eagerly forward to the dinner ever since finding out that her new friend Terrie was going to be there.

It was interesting, Dawn mused: Suzy had identified a family's plane as off-handedly as she herself might recognise a friend's old car. This was an immensely wealthy world, the world of the Kanes and the Austins, and it would pay her to remember she wasn't a part of it. She watched Dan shut down the engine, competent and elegantly casual in a brown corduroy ranch suit. The glimpse of his virile chest through the open-throated collar of his shirt reminded her forcefully that one could—unfortunately—be physically attracted to someone from another world. One could also, if it came to that, be indisputably, unequivocally, and hopelessly in love with him.

Dawn's position at the ranch had subtly but definitely changed. She was no longer merely Suzy Kane's companion, that was clear. The problem was that she didn't know exactly what she *was*. Tonight, at any rate, her role seemed quite clear. As the three of them walked towards the house Dan took her arm in a courteous and proprietorial manner. Tonight, it seemed, she was his date.

The Austins' ranch house was as traditional as the Kanes' was modern. It was a graceful, plantation-style house, partially shaded by ancient oak trees, with wide balconies and verandas. The carved door was opened by a uniformed maid, and they had barely walked into the ornate, square hall when a plump, white-haired woman in a simple black hostess gown burst upon them. Her friendly, unaffected face lit up at the sight of them.

'Dan . . . Suzy . . . !' She embraced them in warm hugs. 'Suzy, I love your hair!' She turned to Dawn. 'And this must be the little gal Duke's been raving about. And now I can see why!'

Dawn smiled shyly and had begun to extend a hand, when she too found herself enveloped in a grandmotherly, violet-scented hug.

'You all come right in, now,' their hostess said with genuine enthusiasm.

Norma Austin was exactly what Dawn had expected. At Dan's house party, Duke had talked fondly of his wife of fifty years, and of how they had survived during the rough early years before the oil strike, working side by side. She was, he had said, 'just about the nicest, most down-home, best woman in this world.' On the strength of a thirty-second acquaintance, Dawn was inclined to agree.

In the vast living room, Duke shambled over to meet them. He slapped Dan on the back and greeted Suzy, then sent the girl off to join the younger guests in the rumpus room downstairs. Turning to Dawn he hugged her heartily. For a being from another world, she was certainly getting a lot of hugs.

'Not only talented,' he said, 'but pretty as a picture, isn't she, Norma?'

Dawn blushed in embarrassment. 'Does he always exaggerate like this, Mrs Austin?'

'There are only two things Duke never exaggerates about—art and beauty,' she replied warmly, although a squeeze of the hand told Dawn she approved of her modesty. 'And you must call me Norma.' She put her hand lightly on her husband's arm and he patted the back of it. It was evident that after fifty years of marriage they were still very much in love.

'Why don't you go introduce Dawn around while Dan and I catch up on the latest news?' Norma said. 'I'm sure she'd like to meet Buck, and I know you're dying to show her your collection.'

There were several couples sitting around the massive fireplace hearth, chatting, drinking, and munching from a delicious-looking array of hors d'oeuvres. Dawn had already met most of them at Dan's party, and she found herself relaxing as they greeted her with evident warmth. Buck Harvey and his wife turned out to be extraordinarily unpretentious people. Instead of being reduced to tongue-tied stammering in the famous painter's presence, she found herself talking to him with ease.

After fifteen minutes of conversation during which Duke shifted impatiently from foot to foot, he grasped her elbow.

'Come along,' he said. 'Got something to show you. Excuse us, folks.'

The long room, lit by massive skylights, was superb, but what was in it literally took her breath away. Magnificent paintings by the greatest artists of nineteenth-century Western America—Remington, Catlin,

Bierstadt, all of them—hung on the walls. Dynamic bronze sculptures of men and horses reared on marble pedestals. For Dawn, it was like being among old friends; she knew almost every work of art in the room, from photographs and reproductions. But photographs and reproductions, she understood now, were pallid substitutes for these vibrant masterpieces. To see the real things, actually to rest her hand on the tossing mane of one of Remington's marvellously alive horses, was one of the great thrills of her life.

She could have lingered for hours drinking in the works of art around her, but Duke seemed to become more and more impatient as they walked around the room. He practically dragged her from painting to painting, hardly letting her pause long enough to see them. Dawn found herself gritting her teeth in frustration, but bore it gracefully. He was, after all, her host, and perhaps he'd give her another opportunity to view the collection with the respect it deserved.

'Come on,' he said, pulling on her elbow, 'let's look at the contemporary stuff.'

But even the wall of twentieth-century paintings and drawings was passed at a dizzying pace, with only a momentary pause for Buck Harvey's evocative, storm-swept landscapes.

At last, with a theatrical flourish, Duke stopped. 'There!' he exulted. 'Now what do you think of *those*?'

For a full sixty seconds Dawn just stood there, dumbfounded, with a stupid look on her face. Next to her, Duke chortled with delight. On the wall in front of them hung two beautifully framed drawings—her own. There was Dan, lean and graceful in the courtyard of the Alamo, and there was Sam, full of robust life, offering Paint his treat.

'They don't look too bad hanging there, do they?' drawled the old man, grinning from ear to ear.

She shook her head in disbelief. 'But they don't belong here, among these . . . I mean they're just . . . just untutored drawings.' She wasn't making sense, she knew, but her mind was spinning.

'Just untutored drawings, eh? Look, Dawn, I'm not saying you don't have lots of room to develop. You do. But look at these others near yours. Do your drawings really seem inferior? Be honest now,' he urged, 'do they?'

Dawn scanned the nearby works—pointedly avoiding Buck Harvey's—and then gazed back at her own. Duke had mounted them beautifully. Each was double-matted, with one mat a mere edge of charcoal grey and the second one wide and cream-coloured, with a bevelled edge. The stainless steel frames were simple and clean-lined.

'No . . .' Dawn said slowly, 'they really don't. But it's the framing that makes them look so competent, isn't it?'

Duke shook his head. 'Framing is important, sure, but you've got to have good material to start with. You've got quite a career ahead of you, Dawn, if you stick with it. I mean your whole lifetime. No collector wants to invest in a flash-in-the-pan artist. He wants to know there's a good probability of a substantial body of work.'

'I'd give up eating before I'd give up art,' Dawn said staunchly.

Duke beamed at her fervour. 'Well, then, little lady, you're on your way. Now that you've got what every struggling artist needs.'

'I do?' she asked, wide-eyed. 'What's that?'

'A wealthy patron, although this here patron's going

to be in mighty big trouble with his wife if he doesn't stop talking business and start hosting.'

Speechless, Dawn laughed, dazed with sheer excitement, and floated euphorically back into the living room on her wealthy patron's arm. As soon as they entered, Dan brought her a tall drink that she mechanically sipped without tasting.

'I was beginning to think Duke was going to monopolise you until dinner,' Dan said. His blue eyes danced with amusement as he looked down at her flushed and excited face.

She couldn't resist telling him about the drawings and the conversation she had just had with her patron. She loved saying the word, even if she didn't know exactly what a patron did for an artist. Whatever it was, she knew it was highly desirable.

'He told me he was going to have them framed,' said Dan. He put down his drink. 'Come and show them to me,' he demanded, pulling her out of the living room and into the gallery.

When they stopped in front of the drawings, Dan dropped his arm around her shoulders as he inspected the work.

Dawn held her breath as she watched his expression.

'Little did I know,' he said evenly, 'when I saw you drawing me that day, how quickly you were going to work your way into my life.' His eyes moved slowly from the drawings to her face. 'And into my heart,' he murmured, dropping his hand to her waist and turning her around to face him.

A sweet weakness washed over Dawn as he pulled her to him. What did he mean? she wondered, her heart beating erratically. Was he finally saying that he loved her? *Loved* her, as well as physically wanted her? His arms tightened, his face came down to hers, and there was no way she could stop herself from rising on tiptoe to meet his mouth. She let her hands creep up his shoulders, stroking the back of his neck, and then fastening them in his thick black hair, while his own strong hands slid slowly and lingeringly along her back. Dan kissed her ardently, hungrily exploring her parted mouth. With a passion that matched his, she strained against him.

Breathlessly he pulled back, looking down at her with clouded eyes. 'Perhaps,' he said, his voice tight and controlled, 'we'd better join the party before I forget myself altogether.' He kissed her briefly one more time, and led her back to the others.

The next few hours passed in a haze. Dan, his manner definitely proprietorial, kept her close to his side. And although she heard herself speak from time to time, she had no idea what she or anyone else was saying, so dreamlike and blissful was her state of mind.

Dan's touch on the back of her hand snapped her reverie. 'What do you say? How do a couple of weeks in Monaco sound?'

'M-Monaco?' She stared at him blankly, looking even more confused. She had come within an inch of saying, 'Is there a Monaco in Texas?'

'Yes, Monaco,' Dan said drily. 'In Europe.' When she still didn't know what to reply, he said with a hint of impatience, 'You've heard of Europe?'

Beginning to recover herself, Dawn said, 'Just because my mind was wandering a little doesn't mean I don't know my geography.' But where *was* Monaco anyway? Wasn't it in the South of France? Could he be serious about going?

'I'm glad to hear it,' he said, smiling. 'The Haagsons

are flying over and will give us a ride, if we'd like. Suzy's raring to go.'

Dawn looked down the long table to see Dick and Carole Haagson, too far away to hear, nodding and smiling at her. Next to them, Suzy and Terrie were looking at her expectantly. Suzy's eyes were as big as saucers and Dawn noted the pained longing on her face. An invitation from a friend was a novel experience for the young girl.

Dawn looked back at Dan and murmured for his ears alone, 'Surely, they're only inviting you and Suzy, not me as well.'

'Don't be ridiculous. Do you want to go?' he asked again. Then he grinned lopsidedly. 'You might as well say yes graciously, because you're going.'

She shot him a quick look of barely veiled exasperation. 'Says who?'

In reply he merely tilted his head and lifted one eyebrow menacingly.

She gave a helpless little shrug. 'How could anyone pass up an opportunity like that?' she said loudly enough for the Haagsons and the girls to hear. Suzy's face broke into a huge smile and she looked expectantly at her father.

Casually, Dan turned to Terrie's mother. 'We're all agreed then, Carole. When do we leave?'

# CHAPTER SEVEN

A DOORMAN in gleaming livery rushed to open the limousine's door and help Dawn out. Dan thanked him with a crisp nod, then turned to speak to the driver in what appeared to be perfect French. Nervous and ill at ease, Dawn glanced back at him. His tall frame, his dark unruly hair, and his unmistakable granite jawline were as familiar as ever, but he didn't look like anyone's idea of a Texas rancher. In his three-piece suit, pale blue shirt, and tie of burgundy silk foulard, he looked as if he had lived his whole life in this dazzling world into which Dawn had so suddenly found herself plunged.

Her gaze shifted to take in the ornate façade of the world-renowned hotel. Graced with marble pillars and a massive, arched entrance adorned with carved mermaid figures, its stately presence was a countertone to the spectacular Casino rising above the square. From the Casino's roof the great bronze angels gazed calmly down on the rich green of the square's formal Boulingrins Gardens. The gardens themselves, with cacti the size of oak trees growing among lush tropical plants, were fascinating. A child of the southwest, Dawn found it incomprehensible that anyone would want to plant cacti in a climate in which bougainvillea, wild anemones, and fragrant citrus trees grew in wonderful profusion.

Dan joined her, giving her a lazy smile. 'You'd better learn not to look quite so wide-eyed, beautiful, and impressionable, young lady,' he said teasingly. 'It gives men ideas.'

'Don't count on putting any of them into action,' she retorted lightly, smiling coolly at him, although her throat was dry with nerves. He simply looked at her and smiled again, this time with a shade of mockery.

To Dawn's irritation Dan had agreed with alacrity to Terrie's proposal that Suzy stay at the Haagsons' villa. Consequently, the 'protection' afforded by Suzy's presence was much reduced. Since the camping trip, Dawn had managed to keep him at arm's length, but it was becoming harder and harder, since—as he had predicted so confidently—she was battling her own desire as well as his. More than once, usually in the lonely pre-dawn hours, she castigated herself for her prudish refusal to let herself drift into a relationship without marriage. With daylight, however, her strength and good sense invariably returned.

As she entered the hotel, her artist's eye took over, drinking in the richness of colour, shape, line, and texture in the magnificent lobby. There were classically proportioned stone pillars and handloomed carpeting, long leather banquettes and green potted plants; all were suffused with a ruddy glow from the art nouveau rose window in the dome.

Dawn barely had a chance to take it in before an attentive staff had whisked them onto the elevator and deposited their luggage in their suites.

Dan tipped them and stood with Dawn in the sitting room of her own three-room suite. 'I want you to take a nap for a couple of hours, Dawn,' he ordered matter-of-factly.

Dawn bridled at his commanding tone. He might have exchanged his Texas look for the style and ease of a jet-set millionaire, she thought crossly, but he had certainly retained his exasperating habit of ordering her about as if they were on the Rocking K.

'It's ten o'clock in the morning,' she retorted. 'I couldn't possibly sleep.'

'It may be ten o'clock Monaco time, but it's midnight our time. A short nap will offset your jet lag.' He glanced at his watch. 'I have some things I want to take care of, and then I'll be back to pick you up around noon.' Obviously jet lag wouldn't dare affect him. With infuriating complacency, he left.

'Orders . . . Take a nap . . . Do this, do that . . . As if I were a child . . . That man is insufferable. Who does he think he is?' she muttered to the empty room, as she set her purse on the graceful antique writing desk at the window. The sunny, cheerful rooms with their gold-and-white French provincial furniture wouldn't let her stay grumpy, though. If she hadn't known she was in the heart of Monte Carlo, she thought, she might have been in an eighteenth-century château. She walked into the bedroom and sat down at the foot of the bed. Suddenly she laughed and let herself fall back onto the pale-gold silk comforter.

He knew who he was, all right. That was the trouble. Dan Kane was a powerful, handsome, and fascinating man who knew how to get what he wanted from a woman. From anyone. And for some inexplicable reason she had attracted him, despite her youth and lack of sophistication. Or because of it, perhaps? Dawn closed her eyes, stretching. Sleepily, she tried to remember what she had been doing this time last year. Washing the breakfast dishes? Cleaning house? If someone had told her she would soon find herself head over heels in love with a Texas millionaire who was probably intent on seducing her—not that she had any intention of letting him succeed—during an unplanned jaunt to Monaco, she would have thought they were mad; downright certifiable and headed for the nearest mental institution. Life was, to say the least, unpredictable.

She moved her cheek luxuriously against the smooth, cool comforter and closed her eyes for a moment.

It took her a few seconds to place the ringing sound not far from her ear. Opening her eyes, she glanced at her wristwatch and was shocked to discover she'd been asleep for three hours. She rolled over and reached for the phone.

'For a girl who wasn't going to sleep, it sure took you a long time to pick up the phone.' The warmth and good humour in Dan's voice set her blood tingling.

Dawn hesitated, then confessed laughingly, 'I'm afraid I went out like a light.'

He chuckled. 'See you in the lobby in twenty minutes,' he said, ringing off.

She quickly showered, then took out one of the new dresses she had bought on a hurried trip to San Antonio just before leaving for Europe. The pale peach, sleeveless dress with its V-shaped neckline and narrow, white leather belt, was simple but well cut. After slipping on her high-heeled white sandals, she inspected herself in the mirror.

An extremely attractive, not altogether familiar woman stared back at her. Her tawny hair, gleaming with gold highlights and full of body, fell to her shoulders, and the peach of her dress and lipstick set off her Texas tan and golden-brown eyes. She wasn't, she decided, quite as lacking in sophistication as she'd been only a few weeks ago. But it was a sophistication that was precisely skin-deep, she reflected ruefully. There were butterflies galore fluttering about her stomach as she left her room.

Dan watched her walk across the carpeted lobby towards him. 'You're lovely,' he murmured in a low voice, his blue eyes fixed on her. 'You look like spring.'

'Thank you,' she said calmly, while the butterflies fluttered more wildly still.

They dined at the nearby brasserie that fronted the square. Their outdoor table provided them with a front-row seat to the never-ending parade of people drawn to this élite and legendary gambling spot.

Dawn followed his suggestion and ordered the bouillabaisse, a Mediterranean fisherman's soup chockfull of lobster, sea bass, mussels, and scallops. It was heavenly, and she could hardly get enough of the fresh, crusty French bread served with it.

'You remind me of myself,' Dan said, smiling at the gusto with which Dawn was eating, 'having my first French meal and loving it.' Wryly, he added, 'Although discovering new food tastes was about the only pleasant experience I had that summer.'

'Were you with your wife?' Dawn asked hesitantly.

Dan shook his head, unoffended by her curiosity. She could see that he thought her interest in his past life as appropriate, and it pleased her. 'I was just eighteen and the trip was a high school graduation present. But it was a disaster; I hadn't learned any of the languages and I knew next to nothing about the countries I was visiting.' He smiled ruefully. 'The proverbial gauche, rich American.'

'When did you learn your French?'

'Mostly in college. I studied languages and history, as well as the more practical subjects like agriculture and business. And although my father expected me to work as hard as any ranch hand during the summer, he approved of my travelling during the shorter vacations.'

'That explains why you're able to shake off that Texas rancher's manner so quickly,' Dawn mused aloud. She took a sip of the rich, fragrant, after-dinner coffee.

'I thought you liked my Texas rancher's manner?' he said in a feigned grumble, giving her a lopsided grin.

She laughed. 'Is Monte Carlo one of your favourite places?' she asked.

'Not really. Unlike my former wife, I'm not particularly attracted to gambling.'

Dawn saw a muscle in his jaw tense and a harsh look flare in his eyes, and she could have kicked herself for her lack of tact. Of course, his wife had lived here briefly with Suzy.

'Why did you come?' she asked softly.

'For a number of reasons,' he answered enigmatically, with a slight frown. She could see his thoughts turn inward a moment, and then he added, 'I thought it would be good for Suzy. Now,' he said abruptly, standing up and signalling the waiter, 'we have work to do before we join Suzy and the Haagsons at the beach club.'

'Work? What work? Where?'

'You'll see.'

They walked along the busy Boulevard Princesse Charlotte until Dan halted in front of a designer boutique. 'Here,' he said.

Dawn gave him a dark look. 'I have everything I need,' she said firmly. She thought she had settled the question of accepting gifts of clothing from him before they left. As she had the first time, Dawn had refused to argue; she simply didn't use his money in paying for the clothes she needed.

'Did you buy a long evening dress?'

'I have a cocktail dress, and that will have to suffice.'

She lifted her chin defiantly. He would have to focus on the one item she hadn't been able to afford.

'That won't do,' he said flatly. 'At some point I'll want to take the Haagsons out for a special evening to repay them for their hospitality, and you'll need a long dress.' He pulled her into the shop without further ado.

Inside, the boutique was nothing like the shops in San Antonio. Elegant, simple, almost austere, it reeked of exclusivity and exorbitant prices. The moment they entered, a tall, elegantly-clad female of indeterminate age approached them, and Dawn was forced to give in gracefully, but not before giving Dan a quick, scathing glance. He returned it with one of ironic amusement.

Within moments two matchstick-thin models were parading a bewildering welter of evening gowns, all of which struck Dawn as being exotic in the extreme. She couldn't imagine prancing around in a gold lamé tunic with matching bloomers, or in the shocking hot pink dress that looked like a tent large enough to sleep six. Fortunately Dan thought so too.

'I think we'd like something perhaps a bit less fashionable, but more feminine,' he said, distastefully eyeing the hot pink tent as it floated off, engulfing the model.

'*Certainement, monsieur*. I know just the dress you would like,' cooed the woman obsequiously.

As she bustled away, Dan turned and asked in mock despair, 'Unless, of course, you saw something you did like?' Shaking her head, Dawn laughed at the expression on his face.

One of the models returned with a concoction of pale cream silk and minutely-pleated chiffon. The saleswoman cocked her head, managing to be both condescending and sub-servient. 'I think you might like the youthful simplicity of this one. And you, *mademoiselle*, definitely have the figure to wear it.'

Dawn gave a little gasp of admiration as the model turned and strutted, displaying the gown. The thin shoulder straps were twisted ropes of seed pearls, and a narrow band, also coated with pearls, separated the Empire-style bodice from the flaring skirt with its gently scalloped hem. Dan insisted she try it on. Feeling as if she were encased in a cloud as the skirt swirled gently around her long legs, Dawn modelled it selfconsciously for him.

'It looks as if was designed for you,' he murmured, not trying to hide the fact that he admired more than the dress.

He insisted she select accessories to go with it: delicate, gold, high-heeled sandals, and a gold evening bag.

The limousine was waiting for them by the time Dawn had dropped off the purchases in her room. Since they had time to spare before meeting the others at the beach club, Dan ordered the driver to take a leisurely, circuitous route so that he could give Dawn a quick orientation to the tiny principality. Leaning back against the upholstery as relaxedly as if they were touring the Rocking K, he pointed out the sights.

'That rocky promontory ahead is Monaco-Ville, capital of Monaco. People here just call it the Rock. The Royal Family's palace is up there.'

'How many people live there?' Dawn asked, gazing at the sheer cliffs rising two hundred feet from the Mediterranean.

'Two thousand or so.'

'Two thousand!' she exclaimed. 'But it's so small!'

Dan laughed. 'About 25,000 people live in the principality as a whole, and it's only eleven square miles.'

Dawn wrinkled her nose. 'Everything's breathtak-ingly beautiful and all, but I'd get claustrophobia if I had to live squashed in with so many people.'

'Be careful,' he teased, 'you're sounding like a provincial.'

Dawn blushed and caught her lower lip between her teeth. Then she gave a little laugh. 'It's no surprise, considering that's exactly what I am, and I can't imagine why you're attracted to me.' She said the words lightly, but her heart was thumping, and it was difficult to meet his gaze.

'I'm not just attracted to you,' Dan answered simply, 'I'm in love with you.'

She looked at him with startled eyes. Love—not want! The words seemed to fill her chest so that she could barely breathe.

Dan put his arm around her and pulled her close to him. He kissed her gently.

'I should have sent you packing that very first night,' he murmured. 'I was angry at your telling me how to run my life. But when I kissed you—just to let you know who was boss—I felt as if I'd been hit on the head with a mallet.'

Dawn made no effort to stem the rising tide of feel-ings. With a muffled little cry she buried her face in his shoulder. 'Oh, Dan, you couldn't possibly love me as much as I love you,' she whispered.

His arms tightened around her. 'Want to bet?' He tilted her head up and brought his mouth hungrily down on hers. She melted under his demanding lips, her mind emptied of everything but feeling. Then Dan pulled his head back. He took a deep breath and said huskily, 'So much for an orientation tour.' She looked up, disoriented, to see that the car had come to a halt and the chauffeur was already moving to open her door.

Lost in space and time, she was barely aware of changing into her swimsuit and coverup in the clubhouse, and didn't really come down to earth again until she found herself standing on a terrace overlooking two freshwater swimming pools and a small beach teeming with chic, svelte, very European-looking people. Dan was nowhere in sight; nor were Suzy or the Haagsons.

'Looking for someone, *mademoiselle?*' drawled a deep voice behind her.

She spun around and found herself looking into Dan's mocking eyes. 'Yes, you!' she said, giving him a happy smile. 'Did I look lost?'

'Very,' he teased. 'But I have every intention of taking good care of you and not letting you out of my sight. Come on.' He reached for her hand and started down for the beach.

Dawn laughed. 'Have you seen the Haagsons?'

'No, but we're a little early,' Dan answered as he adroitly commandeered two vacant deckchairs for them not far from the water. The undisguised attention he paid her as she slipped out of her coverup to reveal her tanned body, barely clothed by the brief bikini, started her heart pounding.

Suddenly shy, she looked out at the sparkling, blue-green water of the Mediterranean, which was whipped into little waves by a slight breeze. Streamlined and beautiful, sailboats cruised offshore, their sails a dazzling white against the burning blue of the sky. Above them seagulls swooped and soared. The only sound was the muted thumping of the soft, curling breakers.

The past and future receded for Dawn. She refused to worry about Dan's intentions. Perhaps it was because too much thought, too much questioning, might burst the fragile bubble of happiness that swelled inside her. It was enough to savour these exquisite moments in his presence.

'I could have throttled you the first time I saw you in that suit,' he said softly, reaching for her hand. 'You couldn't have picked a worse time to turn into a butterfly. I'll probably never live it down.'

She swung her head around and smiled shyly into his eyes. 'You did look pretty ferocious,' she said, as her eyes dropped down to take in the marvellous sight of his hand holding hers, his dark, strong, sinewy hand that contrasted so much with the smooth slenderness of hers. He had taken off his cotton, white-and-red striped shirt and wore white shorts that emphasised the brownness of his skin and the thick, sensual mat of dark hair on his chest.

A covey of bikini-clad girls strolled by. From their chatter and open stares at the lean, dark figure beside her, Dawn saw that she wasn't the only female whose attention was drawn to Dan Kane. It was intensely gratifying to see that he never noticed them.

He looked over her shoulder. 'There are Suzy and the Haagsons,' he said, slowly relinquishing her hand.

Suzy, her brown curls gleaming, and dressed in her yellow bathing suit, ran to greet them.

'Having fun, squirt?' Dan asked, watching his coltish daughter plop down on the sand near their chairs. Dawn could detect a note of concern in his voice.

'Uh-*huh*! Mr and Mrs Haagson are super, and Terrie and I have a great room!' she exclaimed.

The irrepressibility of youth was obviously standing Suzy in good stead. Nothing about her suggested that she was haunted by painful memories of having been here with her mother. Also, Dawn realised thankfully, three years was a long time for a thirteen-year-old.

Terrie joined Suzy on the sand and Dan jumped up to give Carole Haagson his seat, while he and Dick went to pull over some more chairs. Dick and Carole were a friendly couple and Dawn had liked them on first sight.

Carole, a petite woman from whom Terrie got her good looks, sank into the deckchair with a sigh. 'For weeks, I've been looking forward to doing nothing but lying in the sun.'

Usually, Carole put in close to a forty-hour work week fund-raising and doing other volunteer work for Houston's symphony orchestra and art museum. Her soft-spoken, tall and lanky husband had suggested the trip because he felt she'd been overdoing it.

'But Mother,' said Terrie, 'you said you'd take us swimming!'

Carole groaned. 'I did?'

'Let me,' Dawn interjected. 'I'd love to go for a swim.'

'I'm game, too,' said Dan, as he and Dick arrived with two more chairs.

It was a spontaneous and uneven race to the water. Dan won hands down, naturally enough, and as winner got to duck all three of them in the water. The playful atmosphere established during that first riotous swim set the mood for the entire lovely, action-filled two weeks.

The sightseeing schedule was established that night over dinner, with Dan insisting that Carole and Dick spend most of their time relaxing, while he showed the girls and Dawn the sights. During the following days, Dawn found the Monégasques easy-going and jolly people. And with reason; they paid almost no taxes, had no military service, and enjoyed one of the world's highest per-capita incomes.

There was a distinct holiday air about Monaco, and although Dawn knew she would quickly have tired of perpetual frivolity, it was a heavenly place for her first real holiday.

She would have been content to spend days at the Oceanographic Museum and Aquarium, watching the gorgeous and bizarre forms of sea life swimming placidly in the big tanks. But there were other museums to see, and gardens, and even a zoo. And, of course, the lovely afternoons were spent swimming at the beach or sailing in the slender, thirty-foot boat Dan chartered for their stay.

On most mornings Terrie and Suzy would join them at the hotel for breakfast, so that she and Dan were almost never alone. And when they were, Dan was a perfect gentleman. Dawn was enormously relieved; she would not, it appeared, have to do battle for her virtue. On the other hand, a small, contrary part of her sometimes wished she'd have to fight for it just a *little*.

Occasionally, she would look up to find him studying her with brooding eyes. Was it the memory of his traumatic marriage that was haunting him? Was it fear of trusting her? Or was it that against the background of Monaco she seemed lacklustre and commonplace? There was little she could do, she decided, but wait for him to confide in her.

The days, each too short, flew by, and somehow the last evening arrived. It was the four adults' night out, and the teenagers would spend the evening under the watchful eye of the villa's housekeeper. Dawn took particular pains with her dressing because Dan was taking them for a special dinner at the elegant restaurant atop their hotel. There was another reason, she thought, brushing her hair until it shone; she knew instinctively that he was close to some kind of a decision about her, about their future.

She pulled on her lovely, long gown and zipped up the back. Certainly, she looked sophisticated enough to be Dan Kane's partner. Studying her reflection in the full-length mirror, though, she knew full well that it was only a surface illusion. Underneath she was still Dawn Richards, smalltown girl, USA. Only with an effort was she able to keep her hand from shaking with apprehension as she put on her make-up.

When he arrived at her suite to pick her up, Dan's eyes sparkled so much that some of her trepidation melted away.

'You look absolutely enchanting,' he murmured, dropping a light kiss on her cheek.

He, too, was dressed formally, wearing a single-breasted, black tuxedo and a pleated white shirt with a wing collar. A narrow black velvet bow tie and a red silk cummerbund added a rakish quality that Dawn found rather exciting. Not surprisingly, the formality of his clothes suited his lean, powerful body, emphasising rather than muting his sexual power.

'The Haagsons are in the lobby. Ready, darling?'

'Yes,' Dawn said softly, her heart lurching. He had never said 'darling' to her before. Was it a good sign? It must be, she told herself firmly; now stop asking questions and just try to relax and enjoy the evening.

Dick Haagson pursed his lips and gave her a low, friendly whistle when they met in the lobby. 'Dawn, you look great in that dress. Dan, if I didn't have my own beautiful wife,' he joked, putting his arm around Carole, 'I'd be tempted to give you some competition.'

Carole, stylish in a black gown, added a generous

compliment, bemoaning the fact she hadn't shopped at the same boutique.

A window table overlooking the harbour, in which the world's most luxurious yachts lay at anchor, was waiting for them, and bottles of champagne were already cooling in silver ice-buckets. Dawn was so busy looking at the magnificent view and the dazzling room with its sliding roof open to the clear sunset that she was unaware of the attention she was getting. The cream colour of her gown set off her smooth, tanned shoulders and brought out the amber in her sparkling eyes. Her upswept hair gave her neck a swanlike beauty, and few men could resist covertly glancing at the tantalising glimpse of soft, smooth bosom her low neckline revealed. She did notice, however, that Dan's eyes were always on her, openly admiring her, in a way that set her pulse racing and her heart clamouring. And she suspected there was a responsive flame flickering in her own eyes when their gazes met.

The conversation was lively, and the world-famed chef lived up to his reputation. *Pâté de foie gras* gave way to fresh trout stuffed with *fines herbes* and then *médaillons* of veal in champagne sauce. In the French tradition, salad followed the *entrée* and was succeeded in turn by a ripe wedge of Brie served with a basket of crusty bread. Then, when they all claimed they couldn't eat another bite, fresh raspberries in port wine appeared, heaped with chantilly cream. Even the men succumbed. It was a perfect ending to a perfect dinner.

'Now, how about working off this meal with a spot of gambling?' Dan said as he and Dick downed the last of their cognac. 'Dawn can't leave Monte Carlo without a visit to the Casino.'

The moment she walked into the close, smoky environment of the vast gaming rooms she knew she wasn't going to enjoy herself. She was a day person, not a night person, and this wasn't her kind of place. In addition, she was tired from the full day they had had. Perhaps Dan wouldn't want to stay long, she thought hopefully.

'What shall it be?' Dan asked, studying her face. 'Roulette? Baccarat?'

'I think I'll watch for a while first,' she responded, with a doubtful smile. 'It all looks rather confusing.' She looked up at him and sensed tautness, though he seemed cool and relaxed.

He and the Haagsons sat down at one of the baccarat tables. For a while Dawn watched, but she couldn't make head or tail of the game, even though Dan explained it to her, and she quickly became bored.

'I'm going to look around,' she finally told him during the next pause.

'Don't talk to any strange men,' he teased, giving her a handful of chips. 'Go try the roulette table. It's the easiest game—just pick a number.'

Slipping the chips into her purse, she strolled leisurely among the crowd. It was not that she particularly disapproved of gambling, as long as a person set a limit and didn't lose more than he could afford, but many of the people around her looked mesmerised and desperate, hoping for the lucky break that would make them rich. Others treated money as if it were nothing, losing more on a single roll of the dice than her father earned in a year's sweaty work.

She found the whole scene depressing. She had never put too much faith in luck, preferring to set a goal and work steadily towards it. It wasn't as exciting as hitting the jackpot, but one's chances at success were certainly higher, and one earned what one got.

She drifted back in the direction of her party, but saw that they were still engrossed, so she headed for a comfortable-looking chair in a quiet little alcove not far away, where she could sit and relax until they finished.

Whether it was the many glasses of champagne with dinner or utter exhaustion from the busy day, sitting down was a mistake. Dawn knew she ought to get up and walk around, or order some coffee to ward off the delicious lassitude stealing over her limbs. How embarrassing it would be to be caught sleeping like a child who had been allowed to stay up after bedtime, only to fall asleep in the middle of the party. She'd just sit there for another few seconds and then go back to the baccarat table to join the others.

'So there you are!'

Dawn awoke with a start to find a very exasperated Dan Kane glaring down at her.

'We've been combing the Casino for an hour. We were about to have your name broadcast over the loudspeaker!' Irate though he sounded, she could have sworn his demeanour reflected amusement and something indefinable—something other than anger.

'I'm sorry,' Dawn said sheepishly. How unsophisticated and gauche could she be! Mortified, she stood up.

'If you got bored after losing your chips, you should have come and asked me for more,' he admonished her, making her feel even more like a child. Chastened, she opened her purse and wordlessly handed back the chips.

He briefly looked at her with one eyebrow raised, then pocketed the chips, took her arm, and led her back towards the main gaming room.

'I was going to use the chips,' she lied, 'honestly.' He said nothing, just led her severely forward. 'Dan?' she asked hesitantly, opening and shutting her purse in her nervousness, 'You're not going to tell the others I was asleep, are you?' When he didn't say anything for a moment, she added miserably, 'It was such an unsophisticated thing to do.'

'Well, it was certainly novel,' he said drily. 'I've never put a woman to sleep on a date before.'

Dawn's heart plummeted. What must he be thinking? Wondering what in the world he was doing with so juvenile and unsophisticated a woman? With a country girl who drifted dopily off to the Land of Nod in the dead centre of the most exciting place in Europe?

'I see you found our stray calf,' said Dick good-naturedly, coming up behind them with Carole.

Stray calf—exactly, thought Dawn, heartily wishing the floor would open up and swallow her.

'She found herself overstimulated from the gaming,' said Dan urbanely, 'stepped out for some fresh air, and lost track of the time.'

Dawn flashed him a grateful look.

'Fresh air is exactly what I need,' sighed Carole, stifling a yawn. 'I'm ready to go home.'

Dan was quiet as they walked down the hallway to her suite. Awkwardly, Dawn fumbled at the lock with her key, until he took it out of her fingers and opened the door.

'May I come in for a minute?' he asked in that way of his that made it clear it wasn't a question. Without looking at him Dawn went immediately to the large window, as if she wanted to look down on the romantically lit sculptures and gardens of the square below. She stared unseeingly as a lump rose in her throat. What she had once read was true: One's capacity for despair is in direct proportion to one's experience of pleasure. She had been flung from the highest of highs to the lowest of lows in a mere few days. She released a breath that emerged as a sob. Suddenly emotion blocked her throat and tears were coursing freely down her face.

At once warm, strong arms enfolded her and drew her close against a broad, comforting chest.

'Now what's all this?' he asked in a soothing tone.

'You must think . . . think I'm . . .'

'Unsophisticated? Young? Naive?' he asked mockingly.

She could only nod her head and sniffle.

'I do,' he muttered, and when she stiffened in his arms and tried to pull away, he added, 'All those wonderful things. And sweet, and kind, and gentle—a very desirable woman. I can barely believe you're real.'

'Oh—' she began, but was silenced by a kiss that took her breath away.

'I love you, Dawn,' he said roughly. 'And I want to marry you.'

A tremendous tidal wave of happiness flowed over her, setting her pulse racing wildly. Marriage! She could scarcely believe her ears as she looked up to see him looking enigmatically into her luminous eyes. But the tide began to recede a little as she read the reservations in his face.

'But I need time. At least a year.'

Happiness welled up inside again. 'I don't mind a long engagement.'

'No. I want a trial marriage.'

'A trial marriage,' she said blankly, pulling away from him so she could see his face more clearly. 'What do you mean?'

'Live with me for a year,' he said, putting his hands on

her shoulders, his blue eyes fierce with longing. 'Then if we still love each other, we'll marry.'

With an effort she drew herself away from his hands and the hypnotic eyes that were weakening her knees and weakening her resistance to something she naturally rebelled against. Dawn pressed her palms against her throbbing temples. Love is mutual trust. He didn't trust her. Therefore, he really didn't love her. It had been only a dream. He was sexually attracted to her, that was all, and when he tired of her, he could simply throw her away. The thought probed like daggers into her heart.

He stiffened, sensing her disapproval. 'I don't think I'm asking too much,' he said, in a voice that was suddenly cold. 'These aren't Victorian times. People live together quite frequently now.'

When she just stood there silent, stricken, he went on. I knew you were old-fashioned and I'd have to make a commitment, but I thought that if you loved me—I mean really loved me for myself—you'd bend a little too.'

'I love you . . .' The words came out dully. 'I'll never love anyone again as much.' He took a step towards her but she pulled back. 'But you don't love me. You probably never did.'

He flushed angrily. 'What the hell do you mean by that?'

'You want me, that's all. You think I'm a pretty toy and you want me. Otherwise, you'd want to make a lifetime commitment. And it amuses you to test me, as if you really intended to make me your wife,' she said, in a smothered voice. 'That's what this whole trip has been, especially tonight, another test. Like the camping trip. You were delighted, not angry, that I was bored with the gambling.'

'And what if it was a test?' he asked in a low, unsteady voice. 'I'm not going blindly into a marriage again.'

Tension vibrated in the room.

'Oh no, of course not; you want a test run. And at what point do you ask your veterinarian to check out my potential as a brood mare?' She flung the words at him. He flushed, his mouth hardening, but she went on before he could say a word. 'At some point, of course, I'd fail—nobody's perfect. And then you could toss me righteously away without a twinge of remorse.'

Now she waited for him to speak, but his words were a long time coming, and when they came they were chillingly flat and stony, as if he were already a long, long way from her.

'I think you've said enough. You're deliberately twisting my words. What you've done is put a price tag on your virginity. It's up for sale for the price of a wedding ring—not to mention fifty per cent of what would be our community property.' His insulting emphasis on the last two words spoke volumes. In his mind only she, without money, had anything to gain from a marriage.

Her face burned with anger and humiliation. She turned and ran into her bedroom, and slammed the door behind her. In tears she threw herself across the bed. Only an hour ago, fearing that she was too unsophisticated for him, she had thought she'd reached the low of the lows. How naive she had been! Despair was a yawning, bottomless pit. She longed to be dashed against a bottom—no matter how deep—if only to know there was a limit to the pain.

# CHAPTER EIGHT

THROUGH the long night she lay sleepless, hoping against hope for a knock at the door. It was daylight before she finally drifted into a light sleep, and then she was awakened by a slight sound at her sitting-room door. Trembling, she lay there with her clenched fists pressed against her cheeks, but nothing followed the faint rustle.

An envelope had been slipped under the door; that was all. The note inside was brutally curt and to the point. He had gone to Spain to see a new breed of cattle. He had informed the Haagsons and they would pick her up to drive her to the airport. The hotel bill had been paid. He would be obliged to her if she would fulfil her commitment to Suzy for the remainder of the summer. If he had not returned to the Rocking K from Spain by the end of August, Sam would see that she was paid and would escort her to San Antonio.

She slowly crumpled the note. The future, as barren and flat as a highway through the desert, stretched before her. No, that wasn't quite true. She still had her self-respect and her art, for what they were worth. She'd have to pick up the fragments of her life and go on. It would be worse than useless to torture herself with regret for something that was dead, she reflected, something that had never really been alive. But, she realised forlornly, it was easier to say it than to do something about it.

The trip back to the Rocking K passed in a grey fog, with Dawn somehow managing to act normally. She

wasn't able to fool Sam for a moment, though. When
they were alone for the first time, his kind, weather-
beaten old face saddened, then cracked into a philo-
sophical smile.

'Don't you fret, honey. I know Dan Kane, and I can
guess what happened. After he's had a time to stew and
kick his heels a little, he'll come back to you.'

Dawn gave him a wry smile. 'I don't think I'd better
hold my breath.'

'Well, if he don't,' maintained the old man stoutly,
'he's got the brains of an anteater.'

Sam and Hannah were both of the school of thought
that said one recovered from loss or sadness by staying
busy, not by moping around, and at first Dawn resented
their goodnatured attempts to keep her active. Sam had
Paint saddled and waiting for her at sunup every day
and badgered her into taking early-morning prowls with
him. He was also a great deal more regular than usual in
showing up at the main house for meals, and consider-
ably more talkative. Hannah stooped to a more devious
method. The hardy housekeeper made a theatrical
tragedy out of a cut finger so slight that she would
ordinarily never have noticed it. Consequently, Dawn
found herself persuaded into taking over the jam and
preserve-making and much of the cooking. By the end of
the second week she knew they were right. She wasn't
yet her old self, but she had achieved a degree of surface
serenity and felt as if she might survive.

August melted away. The only communications from
Dan were a few postcards to Suzy. Then, only days
before the mustang roundup—the event that signalled
the end of summer, the end of Suzy's vacation, the end
of Dawn's job and her relationship with Suzy—Hannah
received a telegram warning her that Dan was returning

for the roundup and bringing a house guest.

The housekeeper's kindly face darkened and her lips pursed as she passed on the news to Dawn.

'I see.' Dawn bit her lip. 'Thanks for telling me, Hannah.' Her voice was ominously wooden in her own ears. Just hearing about him—let alone thinking about seeing him in the flesh—shook her hard-earned equilibrium, and he was going to add insult to injury by bringing along a 'house guest'. Not for a moment did she doubt that that meant a lady friend. Well, darned if she was going to give him the satisfaction of letting him know how deeply hurt she was by the entire miserable episode, she told herself with grim determination.

That determination remained formidable until the day of his arrival. Then Dawn discovered that the battle for her composure was going to be harder than she had dreamed. She was alone in the living room, working on a drawing, when she heard the drone of the airplane. Against her will she was drawn to a window to watch the plane taxi to a halt. As soon as it had stopped, Dan jumped down, and there was the familiar catch at her throat. She was as hopelessly in love with him as ever, darn him. At once he turned and helped an elegant, stylish Meg Bronson to alight.

A bitter stab of pain and jealousy lanced her. But he would never know it, she vowed for the umpteenth time, fighting down a wild desire to flee from the ranch house and find some dark hole where she could cry her heart out. Instead, she sought refuge in her alcove and began working again. Dimly, she heard the muffled greetings in the hall, and then the sounds of Hannah and Suzy taking Meg to a guest room.

She didn't know what it was that alerted her to his presence, but she knew he was there in the living room with her. A cold fist turned in the pit of her stomach. She looked up slowly, pale and unsettled. Dan's tall frame loomed above her; darkly silent, with icy blue eyes, he stared down at her.

Dawn's gaze wavered and then dropped. For a long moment she couldn't speak. His mere presence shredded the fabric of her composure. When she at last found her voice, she managed the semblance of a cool tone. 'Did you enjoy Spain?'

'It was interesting,' he answered lazily, 'and the company was amusing.'

Colour rose to her cheeks. 'How nice,' she said almost inaudibly.

'Yes, Meg did a marvellous job of consoling me.' He was expressionless.

Her colour deepened and Dawn dug her nails into the palms of her hands. Anger flared. 'You knew I'd be gone from here in just a few days. How could you be cruel enough to come back now and bring her with you?'

Dan lifted a shoulder in an idle shrug. 'You'd have had to meet us together some time.'

She stared unseeing at her work table. His casual reference to himself and Meg as a pair wasn't the least of his cruelties. Dawn felt tears welling up and dammed them back with raw force of will.

'That's not true,' she replied tonelessly. 'I don't move in your world. I never will.'

Dan laughed without humour. 'Duke Austin won't let you go back to being an undiscovered art student. I imagine it will be my misfortune to stumble over you quite a bit in the future.'

'Well, you don't have to stumble over me this week,' she cried bitterly, jumping up to leave.

Dan clasped her wrist in a grip of iron, then easily

caught the other when she lashed out to hit him. Forcing her hands behind her back, he hauled her against him. She hated her traitorous heart for thumping wildly at his closeness.

'Don't start a fight you can't win,' he warned. 'It's time you learned to act grown-up. You're going to control your emotions long enough to leave here when planned. I'll not have you embarrassing me.'

'Let go of me!' she cried. 'I don't have to do anything you say.'

He eyed her dispassionately. 'Suzy's attached to you, and if you leave because of Meg, you'll harm their relationship. Now, I think you care about Suzy—or was your interest in her just your way of getting hold of me?'

Dawn seethed with indignation. She longed to tell him that his daughter had disliked Meg before she'd ever heard of Dawn Richards, but she didn't want to give away Suzy's feelings. The girl was young; they might change. Besides, he did have a point. Dawn *did* care about Suzy, regardless of his shabby implication.

'All right,' she said, 'but I want to leave at the first possible moment.' Her golden-brown eyes were enormous.

'My sentiments exactly,' he drawled, releasing her. 'It's time to change for dinner, don't you think?' He paused before leaving. 'No childish emotional scenes, if it's all the same to you,' he said icily. 'Try to act your age.'

He had gone too far this time, Dawn thought furiously as she went to her room. No emotional scenes, had he said? Act her age? She'd give him more than he bargained for. She was going to be as sophisticated, indifferent, and aloof as a human being could be, even if it killed her. And she was going to look as good as she possibly could, to show him what he was missing.

There was an hour before dinner, and Dawn washed and dried her hair, then brushed it until it gleamed with golden highlights. With care and precision she put on her makeup, using gloss over her plum-coloured lipstick to emphasise her full, sensual lips. The yellow halter-top sundress was the sexiest casual dress she owned, she put it on.

Straightening her spine, she held her shoulders back. Her breasts were tantalisingly outlined in the smooth, close-fitting top, and the full skirt fell from her tiny waist and flared seductively over her hips. Fine. He wasn't likely to think her very childish-looking, at any rate. With her pulse quickening, she strolled casually into the living room. Dan was mixing a pitcher of martinis for himself, Sam, and Meg when she walked in. His eyes narrowed, taking in her choice of dress and her demeanour.

Meg, beautiful and chic in a white silk dress, was sitting near the fireplace talking to Suzy. Her perfect features were marred briefly by a thin-lipped expression of irritation at the sight of Dawn strolling in with unaccustomed confidence.

'Would you like a glass of sherry?' Dan asked coldly after greetings were exchanged.

'Actually, I'd prefer a martini.' She gave him a bright, slow smile, and he glared back. If looks could kill, she would have expired on the spot. Instead, his obvious displeasure with her only added fuel to her courage. Too bad there wasn't another eligible male to flirt with, she thought, taking the frosted glass from his hand.

'Thank you, Dan,' she said softly, adding a slight overtone of seductiveness to her voice. Dan's expression was wooden as he turned and served the others. But Meg wasn't as good at hiding her feelings. She shot Dawn a look of naked jealousy.

Dawn, in turn, bestowed a sweet smile on her. 'Dan tells me you two had an amusing time in Spain.'

Meg did something with her teeth that barely passed for a smile. 'Yes, Spain's lovely at this time of the year.' Then she pointedly turned her back on Dawn to engage Suzy in conversation.

Dawn took a cautious sip of her martini and had to suppress a grimace; the taste was vile. How could people drink it? Looking up, she caught Sam watching her. Without moving an eyebrow, the foreman winked gravely at her. Clearly he was looking forward to some fireworks.

Sophistication had its drawbacks, Dawn relected, glancing back down at the ghastly drink in her hand. But she couldn't possibly not drink it after making a point of asking for it. That would be unsophisticated. She wondered if holding her breath would make the martini taste less revolting, and tried it. It seemed to work. The second sip went down more easily. A few more sips, each tasting better than the one before, had the most novel effect. She felt deliciously warm and sparkly, and quite capable of coping with any number of Dan Kanes.

When Dan came around with the pitcher for refills, she held out her glass. His lean face darkened.

'Drink it a little slower this time,' he muttered for her ears alone. 'Martinis are lethal for inexperienced drinkers.'

'Well, one must become experienced some time.' She giggled softly.

Meg took the exchange for a private *tête-à-tête*. Her green eyes glittered angrily, and the arch gaze she had been levelling at Dan turned into a tigerish glower. 'Dan, darling,' she purred, 'I'm dying for a refill of this superb martini. Do pour me one.'

'Yes, Dan, darling, do,' Dawn murmured under her breath as he turned away.

His rapier eyes narrowed. From his rigid back, Dawn got the distinct impression that she would pay for this tomorrow, but she didn't care.

Hannah came in to announce dinner. Dan escorted Meg and Suzy into the dining room, while Sam with a flourish gallantly offered Dawn his arm. His wise old eyes took in her flushed face and sparkling eyes.

'Don't need to tell you which little filly I've got my bet on,' he drawled, as they lingered for a moment. He patted the hand that was lightly lying on his arm.

'You're imagining things, Sam,' Dawn said dreamily. 'I have no intention of racing anyone for Dan Kane. In fact I wouldn't walk across the street for that . . . that . . . fool-headed mule.'

'I think,' Sam said, 'that's mule-headed fool.'

Choking with laughter, they walked into the dining room.

The room had never looked so lovely. Hannah had lit the many tapered candles in the massive chandelier with its crystal pendants, and the gleaming mahogany table swam with orange reflections. Dawn's chair placed her close to the centrepiece made up of the beautiful, half-wild, yellow roses of Texas.

With her eyes sparkling, with the colour in her cheeks, with her dress of yellow, she was like a beautiful, delicate rose herself—a breathtakingly lovely rose that put the centrepiece to shame.

'You look *so* beautiful near those roses,' Suzy sighed in admiration. Her eyes were worshipful.

Meg was not accustomed to being upstaged. With her eyes glittering like a cat's, she was barely able to hide her increasingly sour temper. Adroitly, Dan changed the conversation to a neutral topic, and as they ate, Meg recovered herself, brightly and most sophisticatedly dominating the conversation. Never once, however, did she address Dawn directly. But if Meg meant her to feel uncomfortable she failed utterly.

Infused with a rosy glow from the martinis and the many glasses of wine Dan was forced to pour because her glass always seemed to be empty, Dawn was content to savour the luscious food. Hannah had outdone herself. A creamy lobster bisque was followed by a whole roast beef tenderloin nested in a garnish of roast potatoes, new carrots, and peas. Dawn smiled at Dan as he expertly carved thin slices of the perfectly cooked, medium-rare meat, but he kept his eyes resolutely on his work. The culmination of the meal was a hot deep-dish peach cobbler with home-made ice cream.

'Hannah, you've outdone yourself,' Dan remarked appreciatively when the housekeeper entered with the coffee in a silver pot, a bottle of brandy, and glasses.

'Daddy, may I be excused?' Suzy asked as Hannah bustled away. 'I'm sleepy.'

'Of course.' Dan looked pointedly at Dawn after Suzy had left. 'Since I know you don't drink brandy, we'd understand if you'd like to call it a night, too.'

'Of course, dear,' said Meg with arctic civility.

In for a dime, in for a dollar, thought Dawn cheerfully, giving them both a wide, glowing smile. 'Actually, since I've discovered I like martinis, I think I'd love to try some brandy.'

The rest of the evening drifted by in a fuzzy euphoria. She had vague recollections of having more than one brandy, of laughing a lot, and of sipping a late-evening Irish coffee at the fireplace. More than that she didn't remember. Or did she? Wasn't there a cloudy, comforting, puzzling memory of warm, strong arms cradling her against a broad chest and carrying her gently, so very gently that she might have been a precious, fragile treasure?

Or had that been a dream?

# CHAPTER NINE

A HERD of buffalo was stampeding through her skull. No, elephants. No, someone was hammering on her door. Dawn moaned and pulled the pillow over her head. Abruptly the sound stopped, but as she was dozing off again the pillow was snatched away. The light made her wince.

'Up and at 'em. We're about to leave, and I'm sure you'd be disappointed if we left you behind.' Dan's voice was repulsively cheerful.

'Go away,' Dawn whimpered, thrusting her head into the other pillow, but he snatched that one away too.

'You look terrible,' he drawled. 'Hangover?'

'What are you doing in my room?' she exclaimed indignantly, suddenly awake. Her head was throbbing mercilessly.

'A better question would be: who put you to bed last night?' He smiled maliciously.

'Oh!' Dawn blushed. A quick check encountered nothing on her but her brief, lacy bikini underwear and the matching wisp of a halter bra. Her colour deepened and she gathered the sheet more tightly under her chin.

'Now get up and get dressed. We're all ready to go, and I wouldn't dream of leaving without you.'

Dawn tried to think, but her brain was like cotton. Slowly she became aware of an acutely unpleasant sensation in the pit of her stomach. 'I feel awful,' she wailed, 'and I'm not going *anywhere*!'

Dan sat down in one of the easy chairs. He stretched

out his long legs and linked his hands behind his head. 'You started this little game,' she said blandly, 'but two can play as easily as one. Either you dress yourself or I'll do it for you.'

Dawn glared balefully at him. 'I hate you.'

He laughed shortly. 'I'll give you until the count of ten to get out of that bed and start dressing. One . . . two . . .'

'Not with you sitting there,' she gasped, then added pleadingly, 'If you go away, I will. I promise.'

'What? And have you lock the door on me?' he drawled, all hurt innocence. 'Not on your life. Three . . . four . . .'

Dawn's cheeks turned pink. She knew without reflection that he'd make good his threat.

'. . . Five . . . six . . .'

Groaning, she wrapped the voluminous Mexican blanket around her, slid out of bed, and dashed for the bathroom.

'Very pretty,' Dan called happily after her. 'Looks like that pink tent we saw in Monaco.'

Throwing him an icy glance over one shoulder, she slammed the door. Vowing never to have another drink as long as she lived, she swallowed two aspirin tablets. Then, donning a long, full robe, she emerged only long enough to gather her russet cords, matching shirt, and boots, before retreating again to dress and brush her hair.

Dan was standing with a glass of frothy white stuff in his hand when she emerged. 'Drink this. It'll make you feel better—a little.'

Obediently she drank it. She couldn't tell what was in it, except that whatever it was tasted terrible. Surprisingly, it did seem to settle her stomach a bit.

'Where are we going?' she asked, surveying him with icy composure.

'To Duke's for brunch.' He smiled unbenignly when she whitened at the thought of food. 'Afterwards, Duke and I will plan for the joint mustang roundup while you women amuse yourselves.'

The airplane stood waiting on the runway in the shimmering heat. It was only nine in the morning and the temperature was already in the nineties. It *would* have to be one of those days, Dawn thought despairingly, trying to ignore the pounding in her head. It was going to be sweltering, probably over a hundred degrees. Never again, she promised herself, never, never, never. Not even a glass of wine.

Meg had a pleasant enough 'good morning' for Dawn, but her accompanying expression of casual contempt was withering. It was obvious that she had serenely crossed Dawn off the list of rivals for Dan. And no wonder, Dawn thought miserably, buckling herself in next to Suzy, behind the other two. She had tried to act sophisticated and had failed wretchedly. Sophisticated people didn't have to be put to bed because they didn't know how to hold their liquor.

Wishing she were dead, Dawn looked out of the window at the asphalt rushing by. Once they were aloft, though, it was impossible for her not to enjoy the endless panorama of sky, mountain and grassland spread out before her. Soon she and Suzy were busy pointing out things of interest to each other.

In the distance Dawn caught sight of a herd of majestic animals gliding effortlessly across a grassy ridge. 'Look to the right, Suzy,' she exclaimed. 'Mustangs!'

'Well, I'll be damned,' Dan muttered, as he too turned his head, 'Look at the big one out in front. It's the palomino. We chased that stallion on the ground for years without ever finding out where he hides his herd.' When the horses disappeared over the ridge, Dan changed course and flew after them. 'This time we'll be able to follow him and find his hideout.'

As the plane approached the ridge, they could see a narrow gully snaking among the hills. Dawn could barely make out the horses, engulfed as they were in the dust of their own wake as they galloped down the gully. Within a few hundred feet the gully deepened into a narrow, sage-brush-filled box canyon. The horses, running powerfully, disappeared into it.

Circling, Dan dipped the wing for a better view. 'Hickok Canyon,' he said, elated. 'Now at least we know where to start looking for him.'

The air around them was suddenly filled with the flurry of wings. White-winged doves, Dawn thought, trying to focus on the darting birds. The noise of the plane's engine must have disturbed a colony of them. There were several loud thumps. Meg screamed and clutched at her throat. As the shrill sound hung in the air, the engine vibrated frighteningly, then choked to an ominous stop.

'One of the birds must have been sucked into the intake manifold,' Dan said calmly, reaching forward to flip on the two-way radio. But instead of the usual static there was dead silence. 'One of them must have hit the antenna; snapped it off,' he murmured, seeming a little more concerned. 'Don't worry, I see a pretty good spot,' he added, scanning the land below them as they lost altitude. 'We'll glide in.'

His quiet voice, full of competence and calm authority, soothed Dawn. Her nerves were steady and even. She looked quickly at Suzy. The girl had tensed, but obviously had the same sense of trust in Dan. Only Meg was showing signs of panic. Her face was grey, almost green, and the knuckles of her hands showed white where she gripped the armrests with terrified strength.

'Now, when I say "down,"' Dan said, 'I want all of you to put your head down in your laps and clasp your hands over your necks.'

The ground moved slowly closer and then suddenly seemed to leap up at them.

'Down!' Dan barked.

The wheels hit with a jolt and the plane bounced violently forward, tipping from side to side over the rough ground as Dan fought to bring it to a halt. There was a sudden, sickening lurch to the left and a horrible tearing sound. Dawn glanced up to see that the left wing had caught in some boulders. The plane tilted crazily, and the next impression she had was of being shoved against the cabin wall as the wing crumpled under them and the plane settled on its left side.

'Now, I wouldn't call that a perfect landing,' Dan drawled as the plane shuddered one last time. 'But it wasn't bad, considering.'

Dawn and Suzy laughed shakily, but Meg was obviously near hysteria, rigid and still as death.

'We'll have to get out by your door, Meg,' Dan said quietly. 'So you crawl out first.'

Meg sat motionless, her green eyes wide and terrified.

'Meg!' Dan said more firmly. 'Out!'

Slowly the redhead moved to obey. She fumbled at the lock for what seemed like an eternity. Thin wisps of smoke were emerging from the engine, and Dawn began to worry about the possibilities of fire or explosion. Meg continued to fumble endlessly, yet Dan made no move to lean over and help her. Perplexed, Dawn pulled herself up to speak into his ear. She would have cried out at the sight of the blood staining his left leg, but he grasped her hand on the back of his seat and squeezed it in warning. His other hand was clamped to his thigh, trying to stem the blood that welled between his fingers. When his door had caved in, he had apparently been thrown against an ugly, jagged, metallic splinter that had been torn from the door panel. More than that, his boot was wedged in the twisted metal under the dashboard.

Biting back her exclamation, Dawn said as coolly as she could, 'Lean back, Meg, and I'll open the door.' Meg, too self-absorbed to be aware of the injured man next to her, dully did as she was told. Dawn reached over her. The latch was slightly jammed, but the adrenalin pumping through her veins gave her the extra strength she needed to release it. She then half pushed Meg out, holding the woman's hand while she dropped the few feet to the ground.

'Now you, Suzy,' she said, turning and helping the young girl down. As soon as Suzy's feet touched the ground, Dawn whispered, 'Go throw sand and dirt on the engine, okay? Your dad's hurt and we don't want any fire.'

Suzy complied without a word. As Dawn turned to grope for the first-aid box under the front passenger seat, Dan tried to stop her.

'No. Get out now. This plane could go up like a bomb. Later, if there's no fire, you can come back to help me,' he muttered, as a wave of pain flitted across his face.

'When I want your advice, Dan Kane, I'll ask for it,' Dawn retorted, opening the kit and pulling out a large compress. 'Now you be quiet.'

Dan moved his hand so that she could press the compress tightly against the wound. To her relief direct pressure staunched the flow. She wouldn't have to use a tourniquet, but he had lost an alarming amount of blood. Quickly, she bound up the leg with gauze bandages.

'It's hard to believe a gal who looks as pretty as you could have so many talents,' he teased.

Dawn gave him a brief smile, but fear clutched at her heart. The pallor around his mouth and the beads of moisture on his forehead filled her with a sickening dismay. He might go into shock, if he hadn't already, and she had to get him lying down as soon as possible.

'I'm going to try to free your foot now,' she said.

Even using all her strength, however, Dawn couldn't budge the crumpled metal. Panic began to bubble up in her. She had to get him out of there!

'Look in the toolbox under the back seat,' Dan said through teeth clenched in pain. 'There's a tire iron. Maybe you could use it as a lever.'

'Now that's the kind of advice I need,' she said, squeezing his hand and scrambling back. To her immense relief, it took only seconds to free his foot with the iron.

'There's no chance of fire,' Suzy said, poking her head into the cabin. She was pale and frightened. 'Are you hurt badly, Daddy?'

Dan gave her a wan smile, 'I don't think so, squirt. About as badly as the time Tandy nipped your finger.'

With Dawn's and Suzy's help, Dan was able to haul himself out of the plane, muttering only a single oath when he slid down to land heavily on the ground.

'Dan—you're hurt!' Meg exclaimed, her voice hollow.

'I'll be fine,' Dan said, managing to smile again. 'Just fine.'

'You need to lie down and get out of this sun,' Dawn

interposed, taking one of his arms and resting it on her shoulders. 'Meg, you take his other arm, and we'll get him into the shade under that cottonwood tree.'

Dan's meek acquiescence told more plainly than words the toll taken by the deep gash in his thigh.

On Dawn's shouted instruction, Suzy crawled back into the plane and emerged with a blanket and pillow, then ran ahead to spread it out under the tree.

Once Dan was settled in the thin shade with his feet slightly elevated by the pillow, Dawn sat down to collect her wits. Her hands were trembling slightly and her growing anxiety about Dan's condition was threatening to cloud her judgment. But she couldn't afford to give way to panic. Resolutely she pushed her fear into a recess of her mind and tried to analyse their situation with as much detachment as she could. They had flown, she was certain, no more than ten or fifteen miles off the flight path between the headquarters of the Rocking K and the Double Bar D, and if Dan had not been injured they need have done nothing but wait to be rescued. Duke would be in the air searching as soon as they failed to show up.

But now they couldn't afford to wait. Although Dawn's knowledge of first aid was rudimentary, she knew shock was dangerous, and she didn't know if Dan's was severe or not, but she wasn't taking any chances. Besides, he had lost a great deal of blood. If she hiked back towards the flight path, she might be able to signal Duke's plane, indicating the direction in which they had gone down. It could save hours of searching, and hours might mean Dan's life.

Taking Suzy aside, Dawn explained her plan.

The girl listened with frightened eyes. 'Dawn, it's so hot. You'll die of sunstroke or something.'

'No way,' Dawn said lightly. 'Remember, I was raised in Arizona. We get temperatures like this for weeks on end. I'm used to it.' She didn't bother to add that Arizonans were smart enough to stay indoors when it got as hot as this. 'Besides, chances are I won't have to walk more than five or six miles. And I'll wear your Dad's hat.'

Suzy looked dubious but comforted.

'All right, then. You and Meg need to mark a big 'X' on the ground, big enough to be seen from the air. Then stay in the shade. I'll take one of the signal mirrors and you take the other.'

'Okay,' Suzy agreed. 'I'll tell Dad.'

'No, he'll just worry.'

'But what if he asks where you are?'

'Tell him I'm scouting around a little and I'll be right back. Tell Meg the same thing. She seems to have fallen more or less apart,' Dawn said, glancing back to where Meg sat, looking listlessly down at her feet and not offering to help. 'You'll have to sort of take care of her too, honey. Can you do that?'

Suzy rallied and gave a little grin. 'This is what always happens in my books. Beautiful woman collapses in helpless heap—except for you, that is.'

Dawn gave her a wry grin. 'Well, if the plane had landed in a snake pit, it would have been a different story.' She was happy to see Suzy giggle. 'By the way, you're pretty nice to have around in a crisis. Your dad's going to be proud of you.' Dawn gave her a quick hug.

Walking out of the shade of the cottonwood into the blazing sun was like walking into a furnace. It was now well over a hundred degrees. She got Dan's Stetson and a long-sleeved jacket out of the plane and put them on. While the jacket made her feel still hotter, she knew it

would slow the evaporation of body moisture and prevent sunburn.

The first couple of miles were not difficult, except
that, with every step she took away from Dan, her fear
seemed to rise higher in her throat. But she was able to
maintain a steady pace, hugging the gully, her ears alert
for the slightest hint of an engine. But there were no
sounds, save the occasional chirp of a sage sparrow
coming from deep within the brush. The other wild
creatures had also retreated into shady haunts to wait
out the blistering sun.

At least there aren't any snakes abroad, Dawn
thought, trying to distract herself from her growing
thirst. Her mouth felt increasingly dry and her tongue
seemed to be thickening. She glanced at her watch and
discovered she'd only been out forty-five minutes. A
weary hour later, trudging under that solid canopy of
harsh blue, she found her lungs burning and her legs
growing leaden. She was nauseated and headachy too,
but this she attributed to her anxiety and the insane
drinking of the night before. The sun was a flat circle,
brassy and blinding, sending waves of heat that radiated
from the rocky ground, and weirdly distorting the distant hills.

She was finally forced to sit in the scanty shade of a
mesquite tree for a while. There she quickly scratched a
timetable in the sandy dirt to keep her mind off the
panicky thoughts that threatened to overwhelm her.

They had left the Rocking K at nine. Duke would have
expected them to arrive at nine-thirty or ten. By ten-
thirty he would have called the Rocking K and would
have been alarmed to find out they'd left an hour and a
half before. He would certainly have got quickly into his
own plane and flown over the direct flight path at . . . say

a quarter to eleven. That was half an hour ago. Meanwhile, Sam would have called in a State Highway Patrol rescue helicopter. So help must be already on the way. And with luck they would start their search in this direction. No, she reflected in despair, if that were the case she'd have seen them by now. Well, they'd probably look here next, she thought, trying to keep her spirits up.

The rest gave her a second wind and she made better time for a while. But the leaden drag on her legs and the dry, furnace-like heat in her lungs returned in a frighteningly short time. She began to perspire freely, and her skin grew clammy and unhealthily chilled. But, she told herself, she came from several generations of pioneer stock. She wasn't going to let a little warm weather stop her, and she continued to walk on.

Dan's injury had shocked her more than she had admitted. It had shaken her to her roots to see that strong, capable figure so wan and helpless, reduced to dependence on someone else—on *her*. And she wouldn't fail him. She'd come through, no matter what. It didn't matter that he had transferred his affections to Meg; it didn't matter at all. All that mattered was that he should be all right. The thought of a world without Dan Kane—existing somewhere, even if not at her side—was too devastating to be borne.

Common sense still told her that apprehension and worry would drain her of needed strength. But now, with her psychological defences crumbling, her fear reigned unchecked.

Dawn shook her head, trying to clear the thoughts away. They weren't doing any good. He needed her *help*, not her maudlin fears; needed it desperately. Doggedly, she stumbled on under the broiling sun. The hat seemed to be gone; she must have left it under the mesquite. But it was too late to go back for it. She had to keep pressing on. Time began to stretch and bend weirdly, so that a single, agonising step might take an hour, but then she would float from ridge to distant ridge in a flash, with no memory of elapsed time. Every breath was like drawing live flame into her lungs, and her throat was closed with incredible thirst, blocked as if with dry, dusty rags.

When the faint whine finally penetrated her mind, she thought at first it was a horse-fly. Dully, she looked up from the ground. A tiny speck was skimming grasshopper-like, not far above the horizon. A helicopter! But it was achingly far ahead and travelling across her path, not towards her. Clumsily, she fumbled for the mirror in her pocket. Holding it up to catch the sun's rays, she bounced the reflected light towards the helicopter.

'Please, please look this way,' she murmured over and over again, through parched lips. When she had almost given up hope, the helicopter tilted suddenly and swung in her direction. Dawn stripped off her jacket and waved it in the air. If she'd had the energy she'd have jumped up and down for joy. As it was, she was on her knees and barely conscious when the freckle-faced young highway patrol man leaped from the cab and ran to her aid. She tried wildly to speak, but couldn't until he forced a little water on her. After that she managed to croak a few broken words.

'Straight back . . . Ridge . . . Hickok Canyon . . .'

Then the sun seemed to fade to grey, and the world went black.

'It looks like she's coming around,' the cool, impersonal voice said.

Competent, gentle hands were pulling something off the back of her hand—adhesive tape. The hand throbbed briefly, and then the throbbing was gone. Dawn struggled to open her eyes and saw a nurse wheeling away a table with a suspended bottle from which a long thin tube descended. Had she been given fluid intravenously? Why? What was she doing in a hospital?

She realised someone was on her other side holding her wrist, and she turned her head, wincing as a spasm of pain shot between her temples.

A clean-featured, white-haired man with a stethoscope patted her hand. 'That's quite a constitution you've been blessed with, young woman.'

Her memory suddenly flooded back. 'Dan . . .' she said 'Where's Dan?'

'Just a few doors down. He's fine. Don't get excited, now.' The doctor shook his head waggishly. 'A very lucky man, thanks to you. He couldn't have gone much longer without medical attention in that heat.'

Dawn sighed in relief. The doctor picked up a tall glass with a bent straw and held it so that she could take a few cool sips. Never had plain water tasted so heavenly.

'May I see him?' she asked falteringly, as she laid her head back on the pillows.

'I don't think it would be good for him just yet,' the doctor said, chuckling. 'He was . . . ah, somewhat incensed when he heard what you'd done. Roaring mad, in fact, or he would have been if he'd been able to roar.'

Dawn smiled wanly. 'It wasn't a big thing. I'm desert-bred. I can't imagine why I fainted from the heat. I've never done that before.'

He frowned. 'My dear girl, you didn't faint. You collapsed from heat exhaustion brought on by the temperature and dehydration. You might well have died, you know.'

'Heat exhaustion, from walking a few miles?' Dawn asked, puzzled.

'I don't think you realise just what you did. You walked over eight miles in a temperature of 115° in the shade. That was very, very foolhardy.' He patted her hand again. 'And extraordinarily brave.'

Dawn blushed and her hand plucked nervously at the white sheet. 'I didn't realise it had gotten that hot.'

'Well,' replied the doctor, now smiling gently, 'I suspect that even if you did you'd have tramped off anyway. Now,' he said, becoming businesslike, 'you'll be fine, but I think we'll keep you here overnight to be on the safe side.'

'And Dan?'

'Three or four days and he'll be up and around. Not going to be riding any horses for a few weeks, though.'

The nurse returned with a small tray, and the doctor continued. 'After you drink your orange juice and have a snack, there's a little girl patiently waiting to pay you a visit.'

'How are you feeling?' asked the nurse as she set the tray down and raised the bed to put Dawn in a sitting position.

'Fine, I think, except for a horrendous headache.'

'No wonder, after what you've been through today,' the doctor said. 'Once you put something in your stomach I'll see that you get something for it.' After a final pat on Dawn's hand, he left with the nurse.

Never mind *today*, Dawn thought. That gallon of martinis last night hadn't done her any good either. She shuddered at the memory, but the soft-boiled eggs and buttered toast tasted delicious, and the orange juice went down like nectar. She was still hungry when she'd finished.

When the nurse returned with two white pills in a tiny fluted paper cup, she smiled knowingly at Dawn's scraped-clean-bowl. 'Let's give your stomach a chance to digest that. Then, if you feel all right, we'll give you a more substantial dinner in a couple of hours.'

As soon as the nurse was gone, Suzy appeared, her brown curls tousled and dusty and her clothes dirt-stained.

'Am I allowed to hug you?' She asked anxiously.

Dawn laughed and held out her arms. Suzy gave her a gargantuan hug, and then perched on the side of the bed.

'The doctor says you have the constitution of a horse.' Suzy grinned impishly. 'I think it was a compliment.'

Dawn laughed. 'Have you seen your dad? How does he look?'

'Not yet. They put him to sleep. That gash on his leg took twenty-two stitches to close,' she said, her eyes round, 'and they had to give him a transfusion. He's going to be fine though, thanks to you.'

'And you!' responded Dawn staunchly. 'It's fantastic that a girl your age could keep her head in a crisis like that. I didn't have a single worry about leaving you alone to handle things.'

Suzy glowed at the compliment. Then she made a wry face. 'You forgot, I had Meg. She managed to add at least one whole rock to my fifteen for our 'X' signal.'

Until Suzy had mentioned Meg, Dawn had successfully avoided thinking about Dan's beautiful, wealthy girlfriend. Now the heartache that went along with the thought instantly extinguished her high spirits. But she carefully hid her feelings.

'That's true,' she responded faintly. 'I forgot all about her. Tell me what happened.'

'Well, once we were sighted by the helicopter and I knew Daddy was going to be all right, it was almost fun—you know, really exciting.' Suzy's blue eyes, painfully like Dan's, sparkled. 'Mr Austin had a doctor and a small jet waiting at the Double Bar D, and they flew us here to San Antonio in no time at all.'

'I'm sorry I missed the excitement.'

'Oh, it was a good thing you were unconscious, or Daddy would have killed you on the spot,' Suzy said, giggling. 'He was boiling mad about you doing something so dangerous.'

'I don't know why,' Dawn said, with a faint smile. 'He would have done the same thing if he'd been in my place.'

'He wasn't mad, really—just worried thinking about what could have happened,' Suzy reflected. 'That's the way he looks when I do something dumb, like get lost out on the range. Anyway, Mr Austin will fly us home tomorrow, and then Sam will come and pick up Daddy in a few days.'

With an effort, Dawn managed to ask coolly, 'Will Meg stay here in San Antonio to be with him?'

'I think so,' Suzy said with a little shrug. 'I don't think she's too keen on getting back into an airplane just yet. She says it would shatter her equilibrium, whatever that's supposed to mean.' Suzy made a face. 'Well, I'd better go. Mr and Mrs Austin are waiting to take me to their town house to clean up. All of us get to visit you tonight.' Dropping a kiss on Dawn's cheek, Suzy left.

As the door closed, Dawn shut her eyes and lay back. Slow, big tears ran down her cheeks—of sorrow, pain, jealousy; she wasn't sure which—at the thought of Meg being the one to sit by Dan's bedside. She'd be able to entertain him with her bright chatter, the kind of sophisticated conversation Dawn could never hope to emulate. She'd hold his hand . . .

Angry at herself for crying, she brushed her tears away. All that was important was that he was safe and would soon be well. It was a solacing thought, but it left her a long way from cheerful.

The sight of Duke Austin strolling into her room after dinner was better than a tonic. In he marched, his leathery face beaming, as if he owned the place. (Later she found out he practically did, having endowed the original building fund). Behind him bustled a cheery Norma, bearing flowers, and Suzy carrying a monstrous box of chocolates. After Dawn had happily accepted the gifts and her visitors were seated, Duke delivered some startling news.

'Newspaper reporters have been hounding the hospital for an interview with you.' He chuckled at the surprise on Dawn's face. 'It was quite a heroic thing you did, you know. Of course, your agent thought it would be great publicity, but I vetoed it, knowing you're kind of shy and all.'

'My agent? I don't understand.'

'All artists make a mess of the business end,' Duke explained patiently, 'so, assuming it's okay with you, a friend of mine's offered to handle your work for the usual commission. He's already lined up a one-woman show in a gallery here in town for you.'

Dawn's jaw dropped in astonishment. 'I can't believe it! A show of my work!' It was every artist's dream. She wished she could get up and dance around the room.

Norma studied Dawn's flushed, excited face. 'That's enough business talk, Duke,' she interjected in a voice that brooked no argument. 'There's plenty of time to talk about Dawn's career after she's had a good night's sleep.' She turned back to Dawn. 'Now tell me, how's the food here, honey?'

When the three of them left to visit Dan, Dawn longed to go with them. Just one look would reassure her he was truly all right, but the doctor's orders forbidding her to see him were firm.

Lying back, she let her thoughts drift. One part of her life had come to a dead end; Dan Kane was not in her future. And at almost the same time another part of her life had grown fertile and flowered; she had a career before her, a career she'd always hoped for but never really believed possible.

One door shuts, another opens. The great balancing scales of life. It was too bad, she thought idly, floating towards sleep, that one didn't have a choice in the matter.

# CHAPTER TEN

WHEN she arrived back at the Rocking K with Suzy, something had changed, but Dawn couldn't put her finger on what it was, except that she was being subtly excluded from the activities of the ranch house. At first she put her feelings down to her convalescent status. Hannah was solicitous, supportive, and concerned during her first day back, fluffing pillows, bringing snacks, and generally clucking about like a mother hen, but—something was different.

She was sure of it when Sam suggested at dinner that night that a welcome-home party for Dan might be arranged. Everyone but Dawn was excitedly given tasks. She, Sam cautioned sternly, was supposed to be resting. Still, thought Dawn, returning somewhat forlornly to her room, couldn't even an invalid do something like addressing invitations?

During the next few days things became more frustrating still. Suzy was preoccupied, Sam vague, and Hannah remote. It took a while, but Dawn finally put two and two together: she simply wasn't wanted. For one thing, her position would terminate a few days after Dan returned, and the people at the Rocking K, probably without being aware of it, were already perceiving her as an outsider. And why not? What else was she? She'd been brought in for a few months to do a job, and paid very well to do it. Now she was leaving, and their lives would go on as they always had.

There was something more, too. These people owed

their love and loyalty to Dan, not to her. And Dan had made it amply clear that Meg was to be his woman. That made Dawn a fifth wheel on the wagon, and a potentially disturbing wheel to a convalescing Dan Kane. Listless and alienated, and not yet strong enough for active pursuits, she spent most of the long, dragging hours in her room, drawing, reading, or sleeping. To her further distress no one seemed to mind in the least.

The day of Dan's homecoming was cool and cloudy with a refreshing hint of rain in the air. After rising late, Dawn was dressing when she heard a tap on the door and Suzy entered carrying a tray loaded with breakfast.

'Hannah said you might want to eat in your room this morning,' she said, putting the tray down. Dawn could see that the girl was nervous and had rehearsed the words. 'Everything's a bit of a madhouse because of the preparations for Daddy's party, and she thinks all the excitement wouldn't be good for you.'

Dawn bit back a retort. Was she no longer permitted even to eat with them? 'You're probably right,' she said with a hint of sarcasm. 'Maybe I should take my lunch here too.'

'Good idea,' said Suzy, disregarding her tone. 'I'll tell Hannah. Then you'll be nice and rested for tonight. 'Bye now. I've barely started decorating the living room.'

She hadn't been imagining things, Dawn thought, watching Suzy dash off. Her presence here was clearly not wanted. Why had she been invited to the party at all? Because she was the brave girl who had saved the master's life? Her lips tightened. How embarrassing it was to be stuck here when no one wanted her around. She threw herself down on a chair and blinked back the gathering tears.

Falling in love with Dan Kane was understandable

ny woman might. But what an utter fool she was to
ave grown attached to all these people. Slowly she
ained control of her emotions. In just two and a half
ays—a mere sixty hours—she'd be back in San
ntonio. Now that she was going to study temporarily
ith Buck Harvey rather than attend art school (another
f Duke's arrangements) she could rent a nice apartment
r herself with her bonus pay. She wouldn't be terribly
appy, but she'd get along fine. She had already earned
me recognition for her drawings, and she had an
onest-to-goodness patron who sincerely liked her
ork. What more could she want? She didn't bother to
nswer herself.

Attempting to brighten her spirits, she built a small
re in her fireplace. It wasn't really cold enough, but the
ght of the flames and the lovely smell of burning
esquite wood did cheer her. After a while she managed
 lose herself working on a watercolour of the view from
er window. She'd get those clouds right yet.

It was late in the afternoon when a knock at her door
roused her from the afternoon nap her body had de-
anded for the last few days. With her heart sinking in
dden apprehension, she opened the door to find a tall,
an form framed in the opening.

'Dan!' she managed to whisper, as her heart thumped
ith the excitement his nearness always produced.

'Are you just going to stand there looking at me, or
e you going to offer an injured man a chair?' he asked
 sardonic amusement.

'Of . . . of course,' she stammered. 'I'm sorry.' The
ght of him had made her forget his wound, forget
erything. With concern she watched him sit down with
me difficulty, stretching his injured leg out.

His smile was faintly ironic. 'Not hard to forgive you,

considering what you did.' His eyes went grimly ove
her. 'My God, Dawn, the risk you took!'

She shrugged. 'It wasn't anything.'

'Don't say that.' His face darkened. 'Come here,' h
commanded suddenly.

Indignant at his tone, she stepped back.

'Are you going to make me get up to fetch you with m
injured leg?' he thundered, placing his hands on th
sides of his chair, ready to rise.

Angry at his ploy, yet knowing she wouldn't want t
cause him any physical pain for the world, she walke
over to him and let him pull her down to her knees besid
his chair. He did it gently.

'Don't ever say it wasn't anything,' he said, tilting he
head up to force her to look into his eyes, surprisingl
warm and gentle. 'It took courage, and it took fortitude
Thank you.'

Blushing, and hoping her love for him wasn't plas
tered all over her face, she nodded.

'Of course, your great-great-uncle Jack would have
accepted your courage as natural,' he said, giving her
half-smile. With a pang she noticed that his face was stil
pale under his tan. He brushed back a lock of her hai
and touched her cheek so softly she barely felt it. The
he placed his hand back on the arm of the chair. 'I wan
to show my appreciation,' he said. 'I'd like it if you'd le
me do something for you.'

'Oh, no!' she said fervently. 'You've already done s
much . . . introducing me to Duke Austin . . .'

'I insist,' he said firmly. 'There must be something you
want.'

Only you, she thought bitterly, as tears threatened
Before he could read her thoughts she racked her brain
for something. The thought came from nowhere, but i

as perfect. 'There is one thing. Don't let anyone cull the palomino's herd. Let his colts run free.'

Dan shook his head in exasperation. 'What a foolish little romantic you are. Those mustangs are pests out here. All we do with them is put them up for public adoption.' Then he smiled wryly and shrugged. 'But if that's what you want . . .'

She gave him a little smile.

'You're as bad as Suzy. What happened to the days when women wanted simple things like fur coats or diamonds?'

Dawn was curious. 'What did Suzy ask for?'

'Need you ask?' Dan muttered. 'Never to darken the door of Seaborne Academy again.'

She couldn't help smiling broadly. 'And you went along with it?'

'Of course. Now, will you do me a little favour?' Dan asked.

Dawn swallowed and nodded. What could she do for him?

'Remember the dress I bought for you in Monaco? Wear it for the little party they're throwing for me tonight.'

Bewilderment shone in her eyes as she agreed. 'Sure, you want me to.'

'Good.' He got up, wincing slightly. 'I've brought a few guests home with me, including one that's very special, so I've asked everyone to dress.'

'Oh,' she said softly, dropping her eyes before he could see the pain in them. So he'd brought Meg back too. Was he going to announce their engagement? Or their trial engagement? Meg wouldn't balk at either one, or a trial marriage for that matter.

'I'll leave you to get ready,' he said, placing his hand

on the door-knob. 'You have about an hour.'

Numbly she said goodbye. Dan's injury must hav[e]
softened his brain, she reflected grimly, as she prepare[d]
to shower. Meg wasn't going to be the slightest b[it]
pleased to see Dawn at all, let alone in a lovely gown tha[t]
had been picked out and purchased by Dan Kane him[-]
self.

Just before she was ready to leave her room, Suz[y]
dressed in a blue party frock that made her look r[e-]
freshingly childlike, skipped in, her arms loaded. 'Ha[n-]
nah told me to give you these,' she said, handing her ha[lf]
a dozen yellow roses. 'They'll look great in your hair [if]
you wear it up.' Suzy was Suzy again. Where had th[e]
distant manner gone? 'And it's chilly, so you'd best wea[r]
this,' she added, laying a delicate shawl of antique lac[e]
on the bed. 'It was my grandmother's.'

Dawn looked frankly hesitant. She hadn't planned [on]
putting her hair up, and Dan might not approve of h[er]
wearing his mother's wrap.

'Please,' Suzy pleaded. 'Hannah picked the rose[s]
especially, and I know Daddy won't mind about th[e]
shawl.'

'All right,' Dawn reluctantly agreed, smiling. 'Let m[e]
get my hair up and you can put the roses in for me.'

'You look super,' Suzy sighed a few minutes later a[s]
they examined the results in the mirror. Dawn couldn['t]
help agreeing. She did look 'super.' The beautiful flow[-]
ers in her hair were just a shade darker than the pa[le]
cream of her silk and chiffon dress, and the frothy ski[rt]
swirled against her long legs as she turned to view herse[lf]
from the side. The lacy folds of the shawl, draped loose[ly]
around her shoulders and lightly knotted in front, adde[d]
an attractive, demure quality to the low-cut bodice.

As they walked into the atrium, Dan, breathtaking[ly]

andsome in black formal attire, emerged from the
tudy. He drew in his breath audibly at the sight of her.

'My God, you're lovely,' he said huskily, in a way that
1ade Dawn want either to faint from happiness or to
1row something at him. 'And I'm just in time to escort
ou in.'

Flustered and unsure of herself, she began to protest,
ut he cut her short by taking her arm. At the doorway to
1e living room she halted, dazed. It was packed with
uests and Rocking K hands, all in formal dress or fancy
Vestern outfits. Everyone seemed to be grinning at her.
rom behind her, a man took her arm from Dan,
ho melted into the crowd. Dawn glanced up into the
1ed, sun-roughened face of her father, looking a bit
unned himself, and definitely out of place in a rented
1xedo.

'Dad!' she stammered in shock. 'What . . . what are
ou doing here?'

'Wouldn't miss this day for the whole world, honey,'
e said. 'Neither would the kids.' Behind him, aston-
shingly, were her brothers and sisters. Billy, Joe and
jeorge, looking disconcertingly grown-up, were
1ughing at her surprise, and a nervous-looking Betty
ean, with Louella close behind, pressed a bouquet of
utumn flowers into her hands.

'Best of everything, Sis,' she said, pecking at Dawn's
heek. 'Lots and lots of luck.'

Numb, Dawn almost let the bouquet fall to the floor.
_uck? I don't understand . . .' But, in her heart she did
nderstand; she was simply afraid to let herself believe
. She had no choice, however, when somewhere in the
oom a piano sounded the powerful opening chords of
Vagner's wedding march, and the crowd parted before
er, opening an aisle to a delicate, latticed arch covered

with yellow roses. Dangling on yellow and pale-blu
ribbons, and tied with a gigantic bow a few inches from
the top of the arch, was an antique shotgun. Behind an
framed by the arch stood a ruddy-cheeked minister
bible in hand, attempting to look solemn but failin
dismally.

Keeping time to the music, her bridesmaids walke
down the aisle to the arch, and Dawn's father proudly
and selfconsciously offered her his arm. With her hear
swelling and tears streaming unchecked down he
cheeks, Dawn was escorted up to a grinning Dan.

'I thought Sam's shotgun wedding was a good idea
after all,' he murmured in her ear. 'I may have been a
fool before, but I'm not stupid enough to let you ge
away now, even if I deserve it . . . I love you, Dawn
with all my heart.'

All Dawn could do was smile. If her feet were stil
touching the floor she didn't know it.

'And,' Dan added, 'don't get any ideas. That shot
gun's loaded.'

She was married in a magic dream. If it hadn't been fo
the cool, hard reality of the gold wedding band Dan
slipped on her finger, she might not have believed it was
really happening.

The reception afterwards, brief so as not to tire Dan,
flew by in an equally misty blur. She vaguely remembered receiving congratulations, helping Dan cut the
cake, and moving with him through a stinging shower of
rice to the blessedly cool, dark, quiet courtyard.

It wasn't until they were alone in Dan's vast suite at
the rear of the big house—it was the first time Dawn had
seen it—that she had a second to catch her breath. And a
second was all Dan gave her before drawing her to him.
He held her as if he'd never let her go, raining kisses on

er forehead, cheeks, and eyelids, and then finding her mouth in a deep, long, tantalising kiss.

Minutes later she managed to murmur, 'You should e off that leg and in bed.' She laughed. 'Oops, I think I aid that wrong.'

'No,' he said, 'you're absolutely right. I can't think of better place to be. I'll give you exactly ten minutes to et ready.'

Blushing, she whispered, 'You don't suppose we hould have separate rooms until your leg heals?'

'Not on your life,' he growled, his blue eyes dancing. Now get going. You only have nine minutes and thirty econds.'

Someone had thought of everything, and a beautifully elicate white nightgown was lying at the foot of the big ed. Dawn had just slipped it on when the door opened.

Dan closed it behind him, his gaze fixed on her slender ut rounded body, made more golden still by the soft ght of the bedside lamp. He was wearing a velour imono of deep blue. Her eyes were drawn helplessly to he clean-lined muscles of his chest and the soft mat of air exposed by the V-neck of his robe.

'My time couldn't possibly be up,' she said with a shy augh, as he placed his hands on her waist.

'I got tired of waiting.' He lightly traced the line of her heeks. 'I've been ready for nine minutes at least.'

'Then you can help me take these flowers out of my air.'

He turned her around. She could feel his gentle hands ntwining a few of the roses.

'Was the shotgun really loaded?' she asked with a little iggle.

'Damn right,' he muttered, handing her the blossoms e had removed.

She laughed. Then, in a teasing voice, she asked
'When did you decide you wanted to marry me?'

'Oh, about the time a certain foreman and a close
neighbour said they'd lynch me from the tallest tree in
Texas if I didn't,' he drawled.

Dawn twirled and poked him in the ribs. 'Seriously?'

Dan captured her hand and carried it to his lips. His
eyes darkened. 'I can't afford to be serious—because I
can't bear to think of how close I came to losing you
out there, and how it was my fault for dragging you
along.'

'Not really. I was a perfect little beast the night before
to both you and Meg—'

Dan smiled wryly. 'She deserved it for cadging an
invitation to come back to the Rocking K with me when
she knew I didn't want her to. We'd only met by accident
in Spain you know. She was vacationing.'

'What?' Dawn asked wide-eyed, her heart beating fast. 'But you implied you were going to live with
her!'

Dan looked sheepish, or tried to. It was not an
ordinary look for him. 'I was angry at you for having so
much power. You drew me back to you like a moth to a
flame. And then when I walked in to find you cool and
collected, working away on a drawing instead of pining
for me, I realised you didn't really need me. Or my
money. You were perfectly capable of leading a full life
on your own—and I was the loser, not you. So I guess I
tried to hurt you. I'm sorry, Dawn.'

Dawn looked at him in a daze of incredible happiness
and relief. 'But you were wrong. I *was* pining away,' she
whispered, tracing the outline of his sensual lips with a
finger. 'I just got good at hiding what I felt for you.' She
smiled ruefully. 'I had a lot of practice. But without your

ove there would always have been a part of me missing.'

He looked down at her with a brilliant, almost fright-ning flame of desire flickering in his blue eyes, and his mouth descended on hers. Dawn clung to him, her body matching his passion with her own. He brushed the straps of her gown from her shoulders and ran his hands worshipfully over her breasts. Her body burned.

'But Dan . . .' she barely managed to murmur, as she found herself divested of her gown altogether and pulled down onto the soft comfort of the bed. Struggling with the intensity of her feeling under his kisses and caresses she said softly, '. . . My hair . . . The roses!'

He groaned. With a muffled oath he pulled out the last of the blossoms and the pins. Her hair, in shining waves, was spread out on the coverlet, delicately framing her face.

'Anything else you want me to do before we take up where we left off?' he asked unsteadily, twining one hand in her hair and tantalisingly trailing the other slowly down the length of her to linger lovingly on her slender thigh. He had all the time in the world and he knew it.

Colouring, her cheeks glowing, she mutely shook her head.

'Are you sure? No burning partridges? No other fires to be extinguished?' He grinned, a wicked gleam in his eye.

'Only the one inside me,' she confessed, shedding the last vestige of her modesty. Her body, aching to be consumed, instinctively arched towards him as she pulled him closer, feeling the whole, long, lovely length of him.

He laughed. 'That's one fire I intend to encourage, not douse.'

'I couldn't *stand* any more encouragement,' sh
gasped.

'Want to bet?' he drawled, smiling, and once more hi
mouth found her lips to make good his threat.

# Coming next month in Harlequin Romances!

### 2683   ISLAND OF DOLPHINS   Lillian Cheatham
Instead of being welcomed to the tiny Caribbean island of Tamassee, a research assistant is treated like an intruder in a millionaire's private paradise.

### 2684   NO LAST SONG   Ann Charlton
First impressions are often deceiving. But what can a young musician do to convince an Australian tycoon she is not a ne'er-do-well out to hoodwink his favorite aunt?

### 2685   LOVE'S GOOD FORTUNE   Louise Harris
An art student, heiress to millions, is pleased when a critically-acclaimed painter seems genuinely interested in her and not just her fortune—until he jumps at her rather hasty proposal.

### 2686   LAKE HAUPIRI MOON   Mary Moore
Any man who would even contemplate marriage without love is surefire trouble. So a young nurse pretends she's otherwise engaged when she falls in love with a disillusioned New Zealand sheep-station owner.

### 2687   NO HONOURABLE COMPROMISE   Jessica Steele
All's fair in love and war. And when a business tycoon snatches a place on the board of directors from the company owner's daughter, she plans a major offensive to dishonor him—only to have it blow up in her face.

### 2688   WINTER IN JULY   Essie Summers
Determined to discover the reason for her father's exile from New Zealand, a Scottish nurse goes undercover and unearths an injustice that threatens her future with the man she loves.

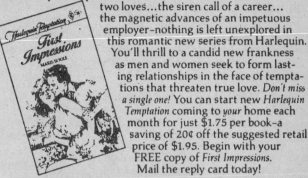